Friend or Foe

Lock Down Publications and Ca$h
Presents
Friend or Foe
A Novel by *Mimi*

Lock Down Publications
P.O. Box 944
Stockbridge, Ga 30281

Visit our website @
www.lockdownpublications.com

Copyright 2020 by Mimi
Friend or Foe

First Edition September 2020
Printed in the United States of America

Lock Down Publications
Like our page on Facebook: Lock Down Publications @
www.facebook.com/lockdownpublications.ldp
Cover design and layout by: **Dynasty Cover Me**
Book interior design by: **Shawn Walker**
Edited by: **Mia Rucker**

Stay Connected with Us!

Text **LOCKDOWN** to 22828 to stay up-to-date with
new releases, sneak peaks, contests and more…
Thank you.

Submission Guideline

Submit the first three chapters of your completed manuscript to ldpsubmissions@gmail.com, subject line: Your book's title. The manuscript must be in a .doc file and sent as an attachment. Document should be in Times New Roman, double spaced and in size 12 font. Also, provide your synopsis and full contact information. If sending multiple submissions, they must each be in a separate email.

Have a story but no way to send it electronically? You can still submit to LDP/Ca$h Presents. Send in the first three chapters, written or typed, of your completed manuscript to:

LDP: Submissions Dept
Po Box 944
Stockbridge, Ga 30281

DO NOT send original manuscript. Must be a duplicate.

Provide your synopsis and a cover letter containing your full contact information.

Thanks for considering LDP and Ca$h Presents.

Mimi

Chapter One
Girl's Night

"Hold up. Hold up. Hold up," Jade yelled excitedly, waving her hand to get her friends to be quiet. Everybody was talking over each other, and Jade was trying to get order so that she could have her best friend, Carmen, repeat what she had said. All the ladies, four in total, Jade, Carmen, Sasha, and Amekia, had a little too much wine. But for girl's night, it was a must. They held it every Saturday at the home of whoever was hosting. They'd talk about any and everything under the sun. The conversations were no holds barred, and what was said at girl's night, stayed there. Currently, the reason why Jade wanted quiet was because Carmen had just admitted that she had never had an orgasm while being penetrated, causing shock to rip through the group of friends.

Sasha said, "I have to ask you to repeat what you just said."

Carmen, who was obviously a little bit tipsier, giggled and said, "I have never had an orgasm while being penetrated. I need clit stimulation in order to orgasm."

Amekia butted in and said, "Clit stimulation is all good, but in my opinion, get you the right man that knows what he is doing and, baby, when I tell you it's an amazing feeling, you better believe it."

Jade refilled her wine glass, took a seat on the fluffy floor cushion, and said, "Let me share a quick story."

"Oh Lord. Here this bitch goes," Amekia stated animatedly.

"No, no, no, look. I think if we share stories with Carmen about our first encounter with penetrated orgasms-"

"Girl, hush, with your drunk self. You don't even know where you were going with your point," Sasha interrupted, while typing away at her phone.

"I've come to recognize not all women can orgasm from penetration alone. I've also come to realize that I am one of those women. And I am fine with that. Clit stimulation is fine with me," Jade explained.

Amekia said, "I was one of those women. But, like I said, I found the right man, and he put that theory to rest. Every other night for about a year and a half, I was cumming all over his dick, multiple times in one round. I don't know what it was he was doing, but I enjoyed every minute, second, hour, day, month of it."

"What happened to him?" Carmen asked.

"Chile, that man was married with a slew of kids."

"What?" Both Carmen and Sasha exclaimed. Jade didn't bother to respond. She knew about that dude, and had heard stories about him.

"How did you find out?" Sasha asked.

"Bitch, I was in Walmart when I saw him. I thought my eyes was playing tricks on me. He lived in Albany and I didn't understand why he was at the one in Schenectady. I thought he was by himself, so I began to walk up to him, but a child calling him "Dad" stopped me in my tracks. I stood there and stared as four more kids and a woman walked up to him. He looked up and saw me, and all the color drained from his face. I turned on my heels and left Walmart, without buying the items I went to go get. He called me later that night. I didn't answer, so he ended up sending me a text. The last text that he sent said that I shouldn't even be mad because it was only sex between us, and we weren't in a relationship," Amekia stated.

"The Nerve! I hope you cussed his ass out from here to Tennessee," Carmen remarked.

"Oh, believe me, I wanted to, but I thought about how I would feel if the shoe was on the other foot. I figured that if it was my husband who was cheating, then I would want to know. So, I burned a DVD with every sexual video that we made, including the ones where he was sucking on my toes, and eating my pussy and ass, and placed the envelope in their mailbox."

"Wait, so you knew where they lived? How didn't you know that he was married with kids?" Sasha asked.

"I didn't know. This man was clever and would bring me over to his single friend's crib, trying to pass it off as his own. I had to do a lot of digging to get the address." Amekia chuckled, remembering what she went through to get his address.

Jade jumped in and said, "Tell them what happened when his wife found the DVD."

Sasha turned to look at Jade, and asked, "You knew about this, and you didn't tell us?"

"It wasn't my place to," Jade responded with a shoulder shrug. That was a fact. What one friend told her, she didn't run back and tell the others, unless they told her she could tell them.

"Anyway, he contacted me 'cause his oldest son was the one who grabbed it from the mailbox. He watched it and instead of giving it to his mother, he figured he could blackmail his father. And he did, for several thousands of dollars. Eventually, they divorced because he can't keep his dick in his pants, and she caught him. When the divorce was finalized, she found the DVD that her son was hiding, and watched it. She went bananas and put sugar in his gas tank, and showed the DVD at their church. Of course, he had the nerve to tell me that it was my fault. Thank God that's over."

The room went silent as Amekia finished her story. By this point, their wine glasses needed to be refilled, and what

Amekia had told them had to settle in. It was only nearing nine o'clock and they weren't nowhere near ready to part ways.

"Look, Carmen, let me tell you a sure-fire way to have the best penetrated orgasm of your life," Jade stated, breaking the silence.

"And what's that?"

"Smoke some bomb ass weed."

All the ladies looked at each other like Jade was crazy. None of them had smoked weed in years, due to the lines of work they were in. Jade was a high school social worker, Carmen was a nurse, Sasha, a lawyer, and Amekia was a dental hygienist. So, it was weird that Jade would suggest such a thing.

"Hear me out. Remember when I was dealing with Troy, the bank manager?" Jade paused as she watched her friends nod their heads. She continued, "One night he convinced me to smoke some weed with him. It had been a while since I smoked, and it only took me two pulls to get high. I was quiet, watching a movie on Netflix, until he was done. When he was done, he stood up from the bed and pulled his pants down. He walked over to me and lifted me from my relaxing position, and I was face to face with his monster. Just a nice, thick chocolate stick at eye level. I looked up at him as he looked down at me. Chile, I sucked his dick something like a porn star. In three minutes flat, he stopped me because he was about to spill his seeds in my mouth. He ended up placing me in doggy-style, and, baby, it felt like I was up in the clouds personally seeing the moon and the stars. The sensation that I felt down there was amazing. I came instantly. Next thing I knew, I was cumming again. And these weren't little ones, these were the ones that make you shake. We switched to missionary and he started flicking his tongue across my nipple, and that was all she wrote. Back to back, I was nutting on his dick. My body shook so hard and I couldn't stop cumming. I never came so hard in my life. Just thinking about it got me ready to cum right now."

"Eww," Amekia stated, and casually moved away from Jade, causing Jade to laugh.

Sasha interrupted and said, "I have to agree with Jade. Some of my best orgasms were from when I was high."

"Boom. I rest my case," Jade said. For the remainder of the evening, they went back and forth with their friendly banter. They gave advice to Carmen, hoping that she would take it. Monday was coming soon, and Sunday was their resting day.

Mimi

Chapter Two
Amekia

Every time I hang out with these bitches, I go home drunk, Amekia thought to herself as she was the last one to climb out of the Uber. Checking her surroundings, she took her keys and mace out of her purse and walked up the steps to her house. When she was in safely, she got undressed at the door and made a beeline for the bathroom to take a shower.

"You're just getting in?" A voice boomed over the sound of the water spraying from the shower head, scaring her half to death.

"It's only midnight, Donnie. You know when the girls and I get up, it could run all night. The only reason why it ended this early is because Sasha got wine drunk and started throwing up all over the place," Amekia said, peeking from behind the white and grey DKNY shower curtain. As she thought about her explanation, she cursed herself for explaining. Although Donnie had a key to her house, they were strictly friends with benefits, and she prided herself with never telling him too many details.

"You knew that I was going to be here tonight, so why didn't you leave earlier?" Donnie asked, leaning his massive frame against the doorway.

"Why would I leave my girls just for some dick? They wouldn't dare do it to me, and I would reciprocate the same way. Especially not on girl's night," she responded as she lathered her washcloth with Dove body wash.

"You the one who asked me to be here tonight, remember? I told you I had to start being at home more often, but you the one who was purring all this nasty shit that you were gonna do if I came."

"And you still could have stayed home, but you couldn't resist having your dick up in my warm lady parts. So why you giving me slack?"

The room was silent because Amekia was right. Donnie had a problem with keeping his dick in his pants, but that was no way her fault. Just like he had someone else, she could have easily called up one of her old joints to come through and get her right. Granted, she would have been less satisfied, but good for the night, nonetheless. Donnie had some amazing wood between his legs, and a greater head on his shoulders. She would have been disappointed if he didn't show, but they weren't committed, so eventually, she would have understood. Passing her rag through the middle of her legs to give her vagina a good cleaning, her clit began to throb, and her nipples perked up. Just the thought alone of what Donnie could do to her body made it react in such crazy ways.

"I could leave if you want me to. Cause all I hear coming from the other side of that curtain is sassing me. And you know how I feel about that." Donnie's voice distracted her.

She peeked her head from around the curtain again, rolling her eyes in the process. "Um, excuse me. Did you say that I was sassing you, and that you didn't like it? You know what?" She declared. Standing under the shower head, she rinsed the soap from her body and cut the water off, pulling the shower curtain back.

Donnie's dick bricked up as he gawked at her perfect body.

She grabbed her towel from the towel rack, wrapped it around her body, and began pointing her finger in his face.

"Oh boy," Donnie mumbled as he turned his back on her and began to walk away. Not because he didn't want the drama, but because his dick was standing high through his basketball shorts, and he needed time to get his shit down.

14

"Oh boy my ass. You started this shit, questioning me, and you knew you could have stayed right where you were. I'm sassing you, nigga? You do not get to dictate how I talk. Let's be clear on that. You can go because this shit here ain't what it is." Amekia loosened her towel and began to dry her body off, letting it drop to the floor as she walked up to her dresser to grab her shea butter lotion.

Donnie didn't want to leave. He knew once he got home, he would be going straight to bed. The way Amekia was bending over to apply the lotion to her legs convinced him to stay just a little while longer.

"Amekia, kill all that noise," Donnie stated calmly.

Standing straight up, she placed her hands on her hips and glared at him. She said, "What is up with you trying to tell me what to do? First, I was sassing you, and now you want me to shut up. I can't believe you. And why are you still here? I told you that you can go."

As Amekia turned around to ruffle through her dresser to look for her favorite pair of lace panties, she felt Donnie's hands gripping her waist softly, and his manhood between her cheeks. Instantly, her pussy began to drip, and that familiar throb to her clit appeared again. *Dammit, why can't I fight this nigga off?* His hands began to massage her soft skin, and she just knew that there was a puddle on the floor.

"I'm telling you to kill that noise because I didn't come here to argue with you. I know I may have said some things to make you feel a certain way, but I've been here since eight o'clock. I don't have work in the morning, but you know I gotta go to church."

Amekia raised her hand and turned around to face him. Standing at six feet five inches, she had to strain her neck to look up at him. She was only five foot three. She looked into his dark brown eyes and studied his face. His caramel skin was smooth with a few scars around his brows, due to fights he had gotten into in his youth. He had a strong jaw line and his nose was like Michael Jackson's, before the many surgeries.

"You can leave," Amekia calmly stated as she looked at him. Deep down inside, she didn't want him to leave. She wanted her pussy licked. She wanted him to dick her down, but she needed to make boundaries. They weren't together and never would be, so they didn't need to be going back and forth, arguing like they were.

Donnie looked down at Amekia, analyzing her the same way she'd just done him. He couldn't get enough of her and battled with himself about if he should just leave. They were playing with fire, and in doing so, comes great consequences. Her golden-brown skin had its own natural glow, making it look like she was dipped in gold. Her natural curly hair was in a messy bun on the top of her head. Her eyebrows perfectly arched, and her full lips were glossed. Her small frame was a bonus, coming in handy when he wanted to pick her up and ram his dick in her. His hands left her waist as she shimmied away from him to get to the other side of the room.

She was feeling a bit sober now, giving her a clear mind to the things she wanted to tell him. Naked, she sat on her small sofa that was in the corner of her bedroom, arms folded. Donnie looked defeated as his head hung, like a sad puppy. *My vibrator just gonna have to do tonight. I'm done with the male species for the night,* she thought to herself. From where she sat, she watched as Donnie walked over to her, placed his knee into the sofa, and leaned close to her face.

"You sure you want me to leave?" Donnie asked. He was so close to her that if he moved a centimeter his lips would be touching hers.

Looking Donnie in his face, she opened her mouth to respond. Then she felt his hand traveling up her thigh and in between her legs. Pushing them apart, he rubbed his fingers in her inner thighs, causing her breath to catch in her throat. His hand covered her Brazilian waxed pussy as he slid his middle finger gently over her clit. Her eyes closed and her head fell back against the sofa. Donnie leaned in and placed kisses to her neck, causing Amekia to moan out in pleasure.

Amekia was enjoying the feeling of his fingers massaging her swollen clit. But then she realized, if she fell for this, she wouldn't have any control over the situation. She had to regain the control. Her eyes opened and she looked at Donnie. With his left hand on her pussy, he was massaging the head of his dick, through his shorts, with his right hand. Quickly, she moved him off her, just enough so that she could get up from the sofa and move as far from him as possible. She was determined to not fall for that again.

"Look, as bad as I want dick right now, I'm not cool with the way things went tonight. I think that we should cool down for a minute," she said in a shaky voice.

"Cool down? What you mean, cool down?" He asked, taking a seat on the sofa, every so often rubbing the head of his dick. His manhood was pulsating, and wanted to do nothing but release, but the woman he was trying to bone was making it hard for him. It was so bad that he had beads of sweat forming on his forehead.

"Exactly what I said. I think that things are getting a little complicated and you're starting to lose sight of what this was from the beginning. I've asked you to leave due to you overstepping your boundaries, and you cornered me!" Amekia was grabbing at straws, at this point.

Donnie sat on the sofa in confusion. Giving up on trying to make sense of what Amekia was saying, he finally decided that he would gather his things and head on home. In silence, he did just that, and Amekia watched him, trying not to change her mind.

"If you decide that you want some dick, you know my number," Donnie stated as he headed to the front door.

Amekia threw herself onto her king-sized bed once she had heard the front door close. *I must still be drunk because I have no clue as to what the fuck just happened.* Reaching between her legs, her hand became coated with her juices. Frustrated, she went into her closet and found her pleasure box. She needed to cum hard to get her mind off Donnie, and put her right to sleep. Her Rabbit would do the trick.

Amekia placed the box back where she had gotten it from and waltzed over to her bed. Fluffing her pillows, she got comfortable and spread her legs. Turning on the TV, she connected her phone and pulled up one of her home videos of her and Donnie. Turning the volume up, she watched as Donnie skillfully inserted himself inside of her and moved his hips to dig in deep.

Her hands went to her breasts as she pinched her nipples. Pain was always pleasure for her, and it turned her on more than one person would want to admit. She watched as they flipped into different positions, finally waiting for him to have her in reverse cowgirl, to get her toy. The G-spot and clit stimulation was a guaranteed out of body experience that she knew she needed. She watched through squinted eyes as Donnie held her by her waist and bucked his hips into her.

She'd watched this video several times, and she knew that this was the part where he was about to cum. She moved her hips as if she was fucking him, instead of her rabbit. She pinched her nipples harder, and this was the part where he tapped her on the leg to let her know he was cumming.

Amekia watched herself climb off Donnie and get down onto the floor with her legs tucked under her. Donnie stood in front of her, grabbed a fistful of her hair, and stroked himself until his seeds were spilling all over her face. Her body shook as she bucked her hips and moved her rabbit inside of her, almost instantly creating a waterfall. She removed the rabbit just as Donnie was finishing up, and then squirted so hard that it reached the bottom of her bed. Satisfied, she rolled over, not bothering to cover up, and went to sleep with a smile on her face.

Mimi

Chapter Three
School Daze

Jade sat at her desk as she looked through the many files of her students piled on her desk. Jade loved her job as a high school social worker. When she first started working at Schenectady High School, she had her work cut out for her. The students were ruthless, and didn't have any guidance. Most of them came from troubled homes, and the only way they knew how to get attention was to act out. On more than one occasion, in the five years that she had been working there, the police were called because the students were out of control. For the past two years, the high school had a new principal that was the students' saving grace. He was a black man in his mid-forties that came from a rough life on the streets.

Mr. Washington, at a young age, was forced to be on the streets and fend for himself. He sold drugs, and went to jail a few times for petty crimes. He came from a family of drug addicts and alcohol abusers, and no one to guide him. He turned his act around when he was faced with going to prison for a murder he had not committed, nor knew anything about. He didn't even know that it had occurred until he was being put in the back of a police car and being transported to jail. He sat in jail for two years, going back and forth to court, without a good attorney on his side.

He was poor and had to settle for a legal aid lawyer. His legal aid didn't have a clue as to what he was doing, and was fresh from law school. For what it was worth, Mr. Washington had trusted that his legal aid would get him out of it. It took two years, but his legal aid was able to get him out of jail and present enough evidence to prove that he was innocent.

That scare made him straighten his act, and upon release, he got his GED, went to college, and got a degree. Now he was a principal, and making a change with the students.

"Knock. Knock. Hey, Miss Rios," came a voice from one of her students. She looked up from her desk and noticed who it was. A smile appeared on her face.

"Chloe! What you are doing here?" Jade asked.

Chloe was one of her favorite students. Chloe had begun at SHS a little over a year ago, and had trouble transitioning. Her father had custody of her, due to her mother bailing two years prior. From Jade's understanding, she was cheating on Chloe's dad with someone from the town that they lived in. Everyone knew, except for Chloe's dad, and by the time he found out, Chloe's mom was packing her bags.

"Just came to say hi," Chloe responded.

Jade eyed Chloe and asked, "Are you sure?"

"Yes, ma'am. My next class is on this floor and I was passing by."

"Okay. If you need to talk-"

"I know, I know. You're here. Everything has been good, though, surprisingly. My dad got a new girlfriend. She seems nice, and he is happy."

"That's all good. But are you happy?"

"Yes, I am. I have come a long way, Miss Rios, and as of lately, I've been guarding myself to make sure I stay peaceful and happy, and it's working. Well, I must get to class before the bell rings. See you around," Chloe said, and disappeared.

Jade smiled and shook her head. She liked when kids would come to her office just to say hi. That meant that she was doing her job, and it was paying off for the students. Jade went back to what she was doing, and an hour later, there was another knock on her door. She looked up from the file that she was reading over and was greeted by a handsome face.

"Hello." Jade managed to get out.

"Hi. Are you Miss Rios?" He asked, walking closer to her desk.

"I am. And you are?" Jade asked, standing from behind her desk to shake his hand.

"I am Darion Dixon. My son is Yajeel Dixon," he said, taking her hand into his. His hands were soft, and when she had gotten close to him, she could smell the scent of Jimmy Choo Man on his body. She was a sucker for good smelling men, and she damn near slipped on the puddle that laid at her feet.

"Oh yes. How are you? Yajeel is such a good student and person. What brings you in today?"

"It's nothing of emergence or importance, but Yajeel had been talking about you nonstop, and how you have been helping him cope with the loss of his mother, and I just wanted to come up and personally thank you."

Jade felt herself blush, and smiled. She leaned against her desk and placed one ankle in front of the other. She said, "It's my job to help the students as much as I possibly can. And you don't have to thank me. It's what I'm here for."

"Losing his mom was tough for him. They were close, and I didn't know how to help him through it. I must thank you for stepping in and helping because I was pained worse than him, and at times, I would shut him out. I wasn't there for him like I should have been."

"You did the best you could, considering that you were grieving too. Don't be so hard on yourself. Yajeel is a bright young man. I'm sure if you explained your position, he would understand."

Darion managed a small smirk and said, "Thank you. Can I ask for a small favor?"

"Sure."

"Do you think you can like set up a meeting with myself and my son so that we can all talk about this?" He asked with his voice full of hope.

"I would love to, but I'm not the therapist. I'm just a social worker helping kids."

Mr. Dixon looked at Jade, causing her to feel small. To Jade, it felt like there was an electric current running back and forth through them. *Oh, who the hell am I fooling? It's been so long since I've had male attention that his innocent request is turning me on like a cat in heat,* she thought to herself.

Mr. Dixon began to talk, "I know, and I fully understand, but I would like this talk to be done with someone who he is familiar with. So that he could be fully comfortable."

"I get it, completely. Let me work on a few things, and if you leave a number for me, I can keep you updated. How does that sound?"

A smile spread across his face as he eyed Jade up and down. He said, "That sounds perfect. You mind if I grab your number too, so that if there is anything that comes up, I can let you know?"

"Oh sure. That would be a wise thing to do," Jade said, lightly slapping her forehead.

Jade passed Mr. Dixon a slip of paper and pen so that he could write his number down. She passed him her card with her school office number, as well as her work cell phone number. With the exchange of numbers, Mr. Dixon smiled and extended his hand again. Jade wrapped her fingers around his and smiled brightly. Mr. Dixon turned around and walked out of the office just as smoothly as he came in. Jade walked back around her desk and sat down, fanning herself. Her phone rang as she slowly got herself together. She had never been so flustered in her life.

"Jade Rios, how can I help you?" She answered.

"You saw my name on your caller ID, you could cut the pleasantries," Carmen sighed into the phone.

"I'm at work so I have no choice, whether I knew it was you or not, to answer that way. What do you want anyway?"

"Nothing. Wanted to see if you wanted to grab something to eat. I've had a long day, and some food, and a nice drink is on my agenda. Can you take the rest of the afternoon off?"

Jade knew that something had to be serious if Carmen wanted to take the rest of the afternoon off. Carmen was a workaholic, and when she was there, she was dedicated. Jade agreed, and hung up to get ready to leave. Letting Mr. Washington know that she was leaving for the rest of the day for a family emergency, she walked to the parking lot and got inside of the car.

Carmen texted Jade, letting her know to meet her at the Mexican Radio restaurant. Jade knew this was going to be good. She knew that Carmen's favorite comfort food was Mexican food. Whatever this was had to be serious.

Ten minutes later, Jade was entering the restaurant. The smells from the delicious food cooking hit her nostrils with force, and made her stomach growl. She hadn't eaten since before she left for work that morning. She quickly spotted Carmen at a booth towards the back of the place and made her way there. She was already nursing a drink and there was one for Jade sitting across from her. Jade placed her purse on the seat and slid into the booth.

"Um, hey, girl. What's going on?" Jade asked. She took a sip from her drink and momentarily closed her eyes to savor the taste of her favorite drink, a frozen raspberry margarita.

"I needed to get out of that office and fast," Carmen responded.

"Why?"

Carmen exhaled and rolled her eyes. She said, "For one, it was slow. So slow that the doctors were in there playing paper basketball. The females, down to the little old white lady, Charlotte, were in there gossiping. And you know how I feel about gossiping. I heard my name come up. The people that brought my name up didn't realize that I was so close. They were talking hella shit about me."

"What did they say? I mean, what can they say about you that would make you want to leave in the middle of the day?"

"You know the sexy doctor, Mark?"

"Yes. The tall white one with all the tattoos and blue eyes. Mmhm, yes, I definitely know who you're talking about."

Carmen yet again rolled her eyes. That man was fine, and everybody knew it. She continued, "Well the rumor around the office is that I've been sleeping with him. Apparently, I work too closely with him for us to be coworkers. They went even lower and one of those bitches said that she had caught us, a while ago, in his office, and he had me bent over his desk."

"Chile, no they didn't."

"Yes, the fuck they did. Everybody that knows me, knows that I don't even find white men attractive. Don't get me wrong, I can admit when a motherfucker is sexy as fuck, but to say that I'm going to sleep with one, and at my job, no less, would never happen. My mouth hung open as they lied on me."

"And you didn't say anything to them?" Jade asked. She knew Carmen more than any of their friends, and she knew that Carmen couldn't hold her tongue for anything. Not even in the workplace.

"Not one thing. And you know that I don't bite my tongue for nothing. I know myself, and if I would have said something, and those funky bitches would have denied it, I would be out of job right now. My hands would have been the next to talk, and while I don't need this job, because I know I could be working somewhere else getting better pay, I love my job."

"Then what are you gonna do?" Jade asked.

The waitress came up and they placed their order for fried calamari, salsa fries, and mini nachos. The waiter left as quickly as she had come, and they continued with their conversation.

"After I heard them, I went to find Mark so that I could speak with him. Don't you know when they saw us walking together to his office, they were pointing their fingers and whispering. Blatantly doing it, too. We went into his office, and I asked him if he had heard any of the rumors that was circulating. He told me that they had been going on for some time now, and there was nothing that he could do about it, except ignore them."

Jade's mouth opened in shock, and then she asked, "Wait, isn't he like the head doctor there? What does he mean that he can't do anything?"

"My point exactly, and I said that. He said that he liked his staff and that they were efficient, and he didn't want to lose that. So, he chose to ignore what the fuck was going around. He told me that I had nothing to worry about because all it was, was office gossip. That I shouldn't be offended behind it because we both know that us being intimate wasn't happening." Carmen drunk her drink down to the last drop. It may not have sounded serious to most, but for Carmen, this was eating her up. She didn't want to potentially lose her job over a rumor.

"What if you went to somebody above him and let them know what's going on? Couldn't they fire the people involved?"

"You know damn well I don't snitch."

"It's eating you up, and you know it. Or else we wouldn't be here discussing this shit. So, you need to figure something out. Whether y'all fucking or not, it shouldn't be a topic of discussion amongst the office. He's the head nigga in charge, and he should have nipped that shit in the bud once he heard the first rumor. Period. You need to let him know that he needs to do something, and if he doesn't, then you're gonna go above him and get it handled. You know men in general don't like that shit. Especially if it's involving his coins."

Carmen exhaled. While she was waiting for Jade to arrive, she had thought repeatedly that she was just being over dramatic about the situation. As she thought further about it, she wasn't being overdramatic. She reacted the way she was supposed to, and Jade was right, she knew that she had to go higher. Mark was her boss and he did nothing, so now it was time to fight dirty.

She spoke, "Girl, you always know how to make me feel better. While I don't want to do this, I know that it's going to have to get done. If Mark has admitted that the rumor has been going on, then who knows how long this rumor been around. I think tomorrow I will contact HR and see what they say."

Jade reached across the table and held Carmen's hand. She looked at her and said, "You are a smart woman, Carmen, and if you need someone to have your back, you know that me and the girl's will have your back, no matter what. So how about we get you out of this funk and enjoy this food."

Chapter Four
Married Life

"Come on, girls, it's time for dinner," Sasha called to her two daughters, Alexis and Aliana. The table was set for the girls, her husband, and herself. It was dinner time, and her husband wasn't home from work yet. This had been going on for the last couple of months, and she didn't know what had gotten into him. He would claim that he would be working late, but she didn't always believe him. She wanted to wholeheartedly. But there was something in the pit of her stomach that told her he was lying. She was a criminal defense lawyer, and still made it home on time for her to make dinner and take care of the household. Her husband was a car salesman, and while their days can typically run late, she doubted that there was a car salesman that would be staying later than eleven at night.

"Mama, is daddy gonna join us for dinner?" Aliana, the oldest of the two, asked.

"I don't know, baby. He might be working late, but he hasn't called me to tell me yet. Tell you what, whether he comes or not, how about we eat ice cream and watch you girl's favorite movie until it's time for bed."

"Yayyyy ice cream," they yelled in unison.

Sasha went into the kitchen to fix her daughters their dinner of creamy mac and cheese, corn on the cob, and meatloaf. She brought them their plates, and went to make hers. She couldn't shake the feeling she was feeling, and she hoped that by the time dinner and ice cream was done, her husband would be home, and she would feel at ease. She had to be up early the next day, due to a new case she had taken on. It was a high-profile case and would guarantee her a promotion with a huge pay raise. Her client, whom was being charged with aggravated murder, was claiming that it was a crime of passion.

Nasir Franklin, known as Nas, was a well-known kingpin, and had kept his nose clean for the most part. Having several businesses to wash his illegal money through, the FED's had a hard time with building a case against him. His workers were loyal and kept their mouths shut, and nobody in the neighborhoods that he controlled would speak. Even though he pumped heroin and crack in their areas, he took care of the people. If there was someone who was facing eviction, he was there, paying what they owed, and even at times, paying for them to stay another year. He was well loved, and if he was gone, they knew no one else would come in and have the compassion that he had. He was out there on Thanksgiving, giving out turkeys and all the fixings, handing out gifts around Christmas time. And for that, he was loved.

Nasir found himself being arrested the night of April 13th, 2018, after he had murdered his wife. They had only been married for a little over a year when she was murdered. He was away on a business trip, looking to expand his laundromat businesses into Atlanta and Miami. He had been gone for a week, at most, and he didn't know how much longer he was going to be away.

Halfway through the second week, he decided to take a break from all the meetings and make a trip home, even if only for a few hours, to see his wife. She was the apple of his eye, and he adored her. Once arriving home, he noticed that there was a car in his driveway that he didn't recognize. Thinking that it was one of his wife's friend's car, he shrugged it off and made his way to the house. With six bedrooms, a studio, and three bathrooms, his house was spacious, and he heard no signs of his wife.

Slowly he walked around the first level of his home, and didn't see her. He headed to the second floor. There were four bedrooms on that level, and he came up empty handed when he had checked those bedrooms. He faintly heard music playing and instantly he thought she could be on the third floor. She was a painter, and with that in mind, Nas had made sure that that she had enough space to be creative. So, he had two of the bedrooms knocked down to make one. For sure that was where he knew his wife and friend were.

As he got closer, he realized that the music was coming from the only other bedroom in the house, other than the studio. He moved in that direction and went to grab the doorknob. Instinctively, he slowly turned the doorknob, as to not disturb her and her friend, he slightly opened the door and peeked inside. As gangsta, ruthless, and deadly as Nas was, and he was, the scene that he saw through that tiny crack in the door would drive any man crazy. Temporarily, that's what it had done to Nas. Reaching into the small of his back, he grabbed his SIG Sauer P228 and pushed the door open further.

His wife had her feet planted on the bed on either side of a light skinned man, who was naked all the way down to his feet. Nas aimed his gun fiercely back and forth between them as they carried on without a care in the world. Nas noticed that the Bluetooth speaker that was playing music sat on a dresser along with a small handheld camera with the recording light on. This infuriated him even more as he snatched both the speaker and the camera and smashed them into the floor. His wife stopped bouncing long enough to look behind her and see what the noise was. As she jumped off her side piece, he aimed the gun at her. Next thing that Nas could remember was that he was sitting on the floor next to their bodies, and he was holding onto her, trying to stop the bleeding.

This case, for Sasha, was a life changer. She was great at her job, but if she could get Nas off and prove that it was a crime of passion, she would have a new office and a salary that would put her in the six figures. There was no doubt in her mind that she would make this happen, and land her law firm, Felderman & Goldberg, a lot of exposure.

After the girl's had dinner, they all enjoyed some ice cream, and Sasha sent them to get ready for bed while she cleaned up. The time was nearing nine o' clock, and there still was no sign of her husband, not even a text message. Making sure her downstairs was spic and span, she made her way to her room. She decided to shower before she climbed into bed to look over Nasir's case. Walking into her bathroom, she stopped in front of the wide, full-length mirror and slowly took her clothes off. She wondered where they had gone wrong to have issues with communication.

One would think that it could have been after her having the girl's she had let herself go, but that was the total opposite. She kept herself fit by attending the gym her office provided on her lunch breaks. No one could tell that she had two kids with how flat her stomach was. She was a far cry from ugly, so she knew it wasn't that. Her ass was nice and plump, and her titties were still perky, even after breastfeeding. Shaking her head, she stopped obsessing over something she wasn't even sure was going on. Their communication wasn't great, but that didn't mean that he was cheating.

Climbing into the shower, after making sure the water was to her liking, she grabbed her rag and lathered up with a brown sugar scrub body wash. She had gotten lost as she thought about the last time she had sex with her husband. It had been a few weeks, and it was the best sex they'd had in a long while.

A smile appeared on her face as she dragged her hand from the middle of her breast, down her stomach, down to her vagina, and in between her lips. Swirling her fingers in a clockwise method, she dropped her soapy rag and cupped her nipple in her hand. She pictured them in multiple positions that they had never tried as he long stroked her, causing her to drip wetness. A cool breeze brought her out of her trance as she opened her eyes. Her husband was naked, climbing into the shower. His dick was rock hard, and before she could give him an earful, he forcefully bent her over at the waist and slid inside of her. Holding onto her shoulders, he slammed into her. Moments later, he was taking his dick out of her and allowing his seeds to leak onto her back and down her crack.

Without another word, he stepped in front of her and washed up the fastest she'd ever seen him wash, and then he hopped out of the shower. Her mind was spinning, and this was unusual for them. No matter where they were, he always made sure that he took care of her body and loved on her the right way. This quickie was something new to her.

The water was starting to get cold. Sasha quickly washed up and climbed out of the shower with a towel wrapped around her head and body. When she entered the room, Brandon had his dinner on his lap, and was comfortable, with his back resting against the headboard.

"We need to talk," Sasha said as she rubbed lotion into her skin.

"About what?" Brandon asked.

"For one, what just happened in the bathroom? Since when do we do quickies?"

"Are you serious? What's so wrong with a quickie?" Brandon asked, which further angered Sasha.

"What's wrong with them is that we don't do them. I didn't even cum."

Brandon chuckled and responded, "I figured that you had been in there for a little while before I joined and thought that you had at least released once. I didn't think there was anything wrong."

"You interrupted so, no, I didn't cum. Where have you been these last few weeks?"

"Working late, Sasha, I've told you this."

Sasha sat on the bed with Nas' case file and fluffed the pillows to her liking. She said, "I'll take your word for it, but I know you aren't just working late. I just don't have any proof that you're out doing something more."

"Are you trying to accuse me of cheating?" Brandon asked flabbergasted.

"I'm not accusing you of anything, yet. But I know it's something more than just working late. I'm not one to just go around accusing, especially if I don't have the proof. Just know that when I do, you better be honest about your shit. Or rather, how about you just be honest about that shit right now?"

Brandon stood from the bed with his plate in his hand. So much for coming home to relax and eat his meal. He said, "Dammit, Sasha, I'm not out here doing nothing. I can't work late without you thinking that I'm fucking around on you?"

"Lower your voice, the girls are sleep. And act like you have sense talking to me. I'm not yelling at you. I just simply need to know."

"Need to know what, though, Sasha? Since when I ever gave you a reason to think that I'm out here fucking around on you? We've been married for seven years and I never gave you a reason, why now? Because hours have picked up? Because I'm just trying to make sure that I can provide for my family? This is ridiculous, and you know it." Brandon paused and then his eyebrows raised. He continued, "I bet it's those man hating bitches that you're friends with that's putting that shit in your head."

"Wait a minute now, Brandon, that's not fair. They are my friends, and you don't have the right to call them bitches. They don't hate men for one, and two, they don't even know about my concerns of you cheating on me. I can think clearly for myself, and if I don't have proof, why am I bringing it up?"

"Then why do you feel the need to bring it up to me?" Brandon asked and turned around to walk out of the room.

Picking up a pillow, Sasha threw it and yelled, "Because you are my husband."

Mimi

Chapter Five
No Privacy

After hanging out with Jade, Carmen felt much better. She wasn't a snitch, but if Mark wasn't going to do anything, then she had to take matters into her own hands. The thought of losing her job flashed brightly in her head every time she thought about it. If it came to that, she knew there were other places where she could be hired and make more, so that was the least of her concerns. As she reached her apartment, she sat inside of her car before she made her way inside. Carmen's mother, younger sister, and her three kids were staying with her temporarily. Her mom was having a plumbing issue at their house, and she didn't want to see them out on the street, so she opened her doors.

They had only been at her apartment for three days and she never wanted them to leave so bad. Carmen allowed her mom to have her bedroom while she slept in the spare room and her sister and her kids slept on air beds in the living room. Carmen's apartment was a decent size, but she felt claustrophobic when she was in there. Nothing was ever clean, except her room. Her mother was a neat freak and wherever she was, she cleaned up her mess, unlike her sister, who thought that everybody else was supposed to clean up behind her and her kids. She had been living with their mother since she had her first born, and their mother had no problem cleaning up behind her.

Exhaling, Carmen grabbed her purse from the front seat and made her way up the front steps and to her door. Thank God quietness greeted Carmen at the door. It had been a long day, and the last thing she wanted to do was be greeted by noise. Unlocking the door, she swung it open and went inside.

Instead of walking in, she stumbled over something, and that something belonged to one of her nieces or nephew. She straightened herself up and flicked the light switch that was on the wall by the door. The scene before her tweaked something inside, and she slammed the door shut. Toys were everywhere, there was food laying around, and her sister had the nerve to have some nigga laying up with her, just a few feet away from her kids. That was where she drew the line.

"Ashlyn, get your ass up, and now," she growled loudly. No one moved. Not even the kids. She walked closer to her sister's air bed and yanked the covers off her and the dude. They both jumped, trying to grab the covers back to cover their naked bodies.

"Carmen! What the fuck?" Ashlyn yelled.

"What the fuck is right. Why the fuck does my house look like this? And who is this nigga that you got laid up like this your spot, naked, and not too far from your kids? Get the fuck up now."

Ashlyn was already grabbing for her T-shirt, but dude had the nerve to grab the blanket and snuggle back under. The disrespect! He said, "Ma, you tripping. Niggas is wild tired. Ashlyn, handle that."

Looking at Ashlyn, she thought she heard this fool the wrong way. Ashlyn had a look of apology on her face, but she knew just where this was about to go. Carmen wasn't wrapped too tight, and after the day that she'd had, this was the last straw. Looking from Ashlyn to this reject, Carmen said to Ashlyn, "Why don't you put the kids in the room with Mama while I help you clean this mess up?"

Ashlyn looked like she wanted to protest, but the look on Carmen's face told her if she knew what was best, she better had not. The dude went back to snoring as Ashlyn woke her kids up to go inside of the room with their grandmother. Carmen heard her mother asking what was going on, and Ashlyn told her that she was gonna clean up the living room. Carmen went inside of the spare bedroom, reached for her Louboutin box, grabbed her .380 Berretta, and walked back out to the living room. Ashlyn was off in the corner, and her eyes got big once she saw what Carmen was carrying.

"What's his name?" Carmen asked.

"Please, Carmen. Don't do this. I'll get him out," Ashlyn pleaded with a shaky voice.

"What...is...his...name? I'm not gonna ask you again," Carmen quizzed. Her patients were running thin. She was gonna deal with Ashlyn after she was done dealing with this disrespectful son of a bitch laying in front of her.

"Johnathan," Ashlyn whimpered.

Carmen wanted nothing more than to smack the spit from Ashlyn's mouth. She didn't mind that she had male company, it was the fact that they were naked a few feet from her two nieces and her nephew. What if one of them woke up while they were having sex? What if their mother had woken up and caught them? Carmen shook her head and walked over to the bed that Johnathan was laying on, snoring like he didn't have a care in the world. Carmen, yet again, pulled the covers off him, but this time, she swung the gun, so the barrel was in his face.

"You want to repeat what you said before you thought it was okay for you to slink your ass back under these damn covers?" Carmen asked with a sinister smirk on her face.

"Yo, Ashlyn, get your nut ass sister. All I'm tryna do is sleep," he yelled as he stood up, wrapping the blanket around his waist.

"All you gonna try and do is get your ass up out my crib without a bullet in your ass. And you got two seconds to do it.

Ashlyn, you better let him know that he got the right one," Carmen yelled.

"Please, Johnathan, get your stuff and go," Ashlyn managed. She was in the corner, shaking like a leaf, and Carmen desperately tried not to laugh.

"Ashlyn, where the fuck am I supposed to go?" Johnathan asked as he tripped over his own feet to get his boxers on.

"And this nigga homeless? What the fuck is going through your mind?"

Their mother stuck her head around the corner and her eyes grew at the sight in front of her. She said, "My Lord, Carmen. What are you doing?"

"Getting somebody up out of my house that ain't supposed to be here. Go back in the room mama," Carmen responded.

"Put that gun away."

"No can-do, mama. He disrespected me and my house, now he needs to go. He didn't want to move the first time, so I'm helping him move a little bit faster." Carmen watched as Johnathan picked up his pace and made his way to the door.

"Ashlyn, don't let me catch your ass on the street! Cause if I do-"

"Cause if you do, you ain't gonna do shit, except catch a few of these bullets in your chest. Get the fuck out my crib, and if you know what's best, and you want to keep your life, stay from around here. I don't care if you have people over here, if I see you, it's done for you. Do you understand me?" Carmen questioned.

She was over-reacting just a tad bit. The anger and stress she felt from work and the overcrowding at her house was boiling over and somebody had to deal with it. It just so happened that it was Johnathan to receive it. Carmen didn't put the gun down until he was out of the door. Once the door closed, Carmen locked the door and swung her glare to Ashlyn.

"Carmen, I'm sorry, please let me explain," Ashlyn said with tears in her eyes.

"Explain what? How you were being a whore right in front of your kids? What if Summer or Trinity would have woken up? What kind of example are you setting for them? You'd rather put dick before them? You could have gone into the bathroom. Hell, I wouldn't have been mad if you went into the spare room, but you had the nerve to be fucking on some nigga in front of your kids, and they could have woken up?"

"Carmen," their mother scolded loudly.

"No, mama. You let her get away with mad dumb shit, and I won't tolerate it in my house. She a grown ass woman and can't even take accountability for the shit she does 'cause you right there enabling her with the bullshit."

"You watch your mouth talking to me like that," Mama said.

Carmen lowered her head. She hated cursing her mother, but she was gonna blow up if she didn't say what she needed to get off her chest. Carmen said, "I'm sorry for cursing, mama, but this needs to be said. It's long overdue, and I will not tolerate this type of disrespect in my house."

Ashlyn wiped the tears from her eyes and stood up straight. She knew her mother was about to get into Carmen's ass. Ashlyn used the fact that her mother coddled her to her advantage, and she was ready to tag team against Carmen to turn this shit on her. *After all, who does Carmen think she is, putting my dude out? Granted, we just met a week ago, but he is the best piece of dick I've had in a long while,* Ashlyn thought to herself. The smirk on her face vanished when she noticed that their mother turned her attention onto her.

"Your sister is right, Ashlyn," Mama said, leaning against the door frame.

"What?" Ashlyn shrieked, causing a smirk to appear on Carmen's face.

"You heard what I said. How well do you know that man that was in here? What if he was some type of sexual offender and touched the girls, or even Zahir? What if he was a serial killer? You need to start thinking through your actions before you do something dumb to get us all killed."

"Ashlyn, the kids can stay here, but I'm going to need for you to find somewhere to go until the plumbing at mama's house is done," Carmen stated as she grabbed her purse from the floor.

"Where am I supposed to go?" Ashlyn asked in astonishment.

"You just had a whole nigga laying up in my crib, I'm sure that you can find somewhere to go for another day or two."

If looks could kill, Carmen would be dead by the daggers that Ashlyn shot at her back. Ashlyn looked at her mother as if she would help, but Mama was getting tired of Ashlyn walking around as if the world owed her everything. She was regretting all the codling that she did to Ashlyn because now, it was bad.

"Next time, pick your men wisely. A homeless man can't help you, except for good dick. Start using your head, Ashlyn, and start putting you and these kids first," Mama said, and sulked away from the living room and back into the bedroom.

Carmen didn't want to put her sister out but what just happened had been too much. She locked herself inside of the spare room and hoped that Ashlyn took what she and their mother said seriously. She was twenty-six, had yet to hold onto a job for longer than six months, have her own spot, nor could she keep a man longer than the time it took to get her pregnant. Before the night ended, if her sister was still there by morning, then she would sit her sister down and have a heart to heart.

Mimi

Chapter Six
Truth or Dare

Montell Jordan's *Get It on Tonite* blasted from the Bluetooth speaker that sat on the coffee table at Sasha's house as she got ready to host girl's night. She was in the kitchen making her oh-so-scrumptious buffalo chicken dip, with honey hot buffalo wings, cheesy bacon tater tots, and four pitchers of sour apple martinis, heavy on the alcohol. For the first time in weeks, she had gotten rid of the girls. They were at Brandon's parents' house. Brandon was staying away. He knew that it was Sasha's turn to host, and he knew how they could get, so he decided to hang with a few of his coworkers after work. Jade was the first one to show up, and slowly the others made their way in.

"Yes, thank God it's girl's night. I've been needing this shit all week," Carmen stated as she slipped her shoes off her feet.

"Who you telling? This week has been the true definition of hell," Jade responded.

"So, I'm guessing everyone needs a drink before we begin our festivities?" Sasha asked with a giggle.

"Yes," they all said in unison, causing giggles to erupt.

Sasha waltzed into the kitchen and poured glasses of the martinis and brought them to her girls on a tray. They sat down with soft sounds of H.E.R playing in the background. Carmen was the first to start off about her week. From the gossiping at work, to her sister bringing a homeless dude in her spot.

"Your sister got some balls on her," Jade laughed out.

"Don't I know it? I kicked her out that night, but the next morning when I woke up, my house was cleaned, her kids were behaving, quietly watching TV, and there was breakfast on the table. She apologized to me, but I had to sit that girl down and tell her that she needed to get her shit together. She is too old to be doing the things that she does, and too old for my damn sixty-four-year-old mother to be taking care of her and her kids."

Amekia said, "They are hiring for a new receptionist at my job. Old Darcy is finally retiring. I could see if I can hook her up."

Carmen's eyes ballooned, and she responded, "Would you? Oh my God, that would be so perfect for her."

"Yes. Your sister has the potential to be great. She just needs some guidance. You're my sister, so she's mine."

"You're amazing."

"We only one drink in and y'all on some sappy shit. Let's get this party started," Jade retorted with a swivel of her hips. She turned the speaker up, placed on *Girl Talk* by TLC, and began to twerk, causing all the girls to get up out their seats and follow suit. They danced as if they were in a club and it was packed with wall to wall men.

Two hours later, they were sweaty and ready to eat. And in true girl's night fashion, they decided to play a game of truth or dare. Jade was the first to start.

"Amekia, truth or dare?" Jade said with an arched brow.

"Hmmm…truth," Amekia responded.

"Is it true that you let a nigga eat your booty like groceries while you were on your period?"

Embarrassment washed over Amekia's face as she looked at Jade. Jade knew it was true because Jade was the only person that she told. She said, "It's true."

"Girl, ew," Carmen stated.

"Listen, I just put a tampon in me and bent over. Shit, if he wanted to, I wasn't going to stop him."

Sasha sat up in her seat and asked, "What does that feel like?"

All heads turned to Sasha as if she had six heads. Jade was the first to speak. She said, "Bitch, you've got to be kidding me? You're a married woman, and you don't know what getting your booty ate feels like?"

Sasha looked at each one of them and shook her head. She said, "Brandon doesn't even eat my pussy because he says that my booty hole is too close."

The girls erupted into laughter, embarrassing Sasha. Carmen said, "Chilllle, if that ain't the most childish shit I've ever heard. I've never had an orgasm, but bitch, you better believe a few niggas ate this booty."

Sasha rolled her eyes and said, "This is why I can't be truthful with you funky bitches. Y'all so judgmental."

Amekia said, "Babe, we aren't judging you. We're judging that jank ass nigga you married. If he ain't eating that booty, then what you married that nigga for?"

"Love, something your hoe ass don't know nothing about," Sasha chimed with a roll of her eyes. She got up from her seat on the couch and went into the kitchen to fix herself another martini.

"Bitch, don't be so sensitive. With your childish, non-booty-eating husband," Amekia called back. Sasha knew that Amekia didn't like Brandon. For whatever reason, he had always rubbed her the wrong way. When the opportunity would present itself, Amekia would make sure that she poked fun at Brandon. Sasha sucked up her embarrassment and went back into the living room. Her girls were laughing at her at the expense of Brandon, and she knew that if she showed that it was bothering her, they would take it further.

"Anyway, whose turn is it?" Sasha asked as she sat back down in her seat.

Amekia eyed Sasha and said, "It's my turn, since I was truthful about my shit. Carmen, truth or dare? And if you pick truth, you know that you have to be fucking honest 'cause there was a couple of times where you and everybody else knew that you weren't truthful."

Carmen sucked her teeth and said, "Bitch, get the fuck on. And I choose dare."

Amekia smirked and said, "I dare you to show us the last thing that you've searched on your phone?"

Carmen laughed and said, "What? What kind of dare is that?"

"It's simple and easy. Just to show your friends the shit that you search when you're not working, or around us," Jade egged on.

Carmen exhaled and replied with a simple, "Fine."

All the girl's surrounded Carmen as she pulled her phone from her purse. She pulled up her search history on Chrome, and was immediately washed with embarrassment. *Was tonight meant to embarrass everybody?* She thought to herself. She had forgotten about the last thing that she had searched because she searched it often. It wasn't even a thought in her head, but once she saw it, she knew that they were about to clown her. Starting with Amekia.

"Oohhhhhh, Carmen likes lesbian porn," Amekia yelled out as she yanked Carmen's phone from her hands and ran around the living room. All the girl's whopped and hollered.

Carmen played it cool, even though her face was red. She said, "Y'all act like y'all never watched girl on girl action before. A bitch was curious, so she had to see for herself. For sure I wasn't about to go out there and actually do the do to actually do it."

Jade choked on her drink as she said, "You're right about that. I was curious to know, and baby, the world that I ended up in had me second guessing my sexuality for a little hot second."

"Jade, you can never take shit serious." Sasha rolled her eyes.

"I am being serious," Jade quipped.

Carmen became quiet as the sound of moaning came through her phone speaker. Her face flushed with heat as she heard the last video she had watched play out. Sasha shook her head as the girls immaturely watched the video, commenting as it went along. After a few minutes, Sasha got their attention.

"Can we get on with this game, or finish drinking. This night has turned to the case of being immature, and this is not what was supposed to happen," Sasha chided.

"Okay. Sheesh, get your panties out your ass, grandma," Jade responded.

"It's my turn to ask," Sasha stated. She looked at her girls and decided that she would ask Amekia. She continued, "Amekia, truth or dare?"

Amekia took a seat on the floor next to the coffee table and looked at Sasha. She answered, "Truth."

"Have you ever slept with any of your friends' men behind their backs?" Sasha asked with an eyebrow raise.

Amekia's mouth dropped open and she took a second to respond. Finally, after she noticed that all eyes were on her, she closed her mouth and responded, "Is that what you think of me? Never mind. The answer is no. Anybody I call my friend, I consider my sister. Hell, even if it was just a random female, I would never knowingly sleep with another female's dude."

The room was silent as they all looked at each other. Sasha felt bad after asking her such a question. She did that to get back at her for the comments that she made about her husband. She knew what she did was wrong, but she was in her feelings about the shit that was going on with Brandon and brought it to their girls' night. Soon enough, Amekia was running out of the room with tears streaming down her eyes. The rest of the girls looked at Sasha with confusion etched on their faces. Without having much choice, Sasha got up and went to go check on Amekia.

Knock! Knock!

Sasha heard Amekia sniffling behind the bathroom door, and her heart sank. She didn't want to hurt her girl. Amekia's skin was a tough as nails, and she thought she would let her comment roll off her. Sasha knocked on the door again, and called out, "Amekia, it's me. Can you open the door?"

Amekia unlocked the door, opening it, only to gawk at Sasha with fire dancing in her eyes. Amekia said, "Are you coming to do more damage?"

"No. I've actually come to apologize. I wanted to get back at you for the slick shit you said about Brandon. I know you would never do no shit like that."

"I've always been up front about my distaste for Brandon, so I don't know why you took it so serious. When I went through that shit with that nigga years ago, Jade knew about it before anyone, but it was you who I shed tears with because I was so hurt behind him not being truthful. If I felt bad about a stranger, just imagine how I would feel if I did it to one of my friends," Amekia stated as she used tissue to wipe her tears.

"I know. And I'm sorry. I'm just going through my own shit with Brandon, and I took it out on you. I shouldn't have done that."

"It's cool."

"It's not, Amekia. I could tell that what I said hurt you, and I don't ever want to be the one to hurt a friend. Not intentionally, anyway."

Amekia nodded her head and looked at herself in the mirror. Her mascara had run, and there were black streaks on her face. She chuckled at herself for looking a mess. She cursed herself for letting Sasha's question get to her the way that it did. She thanked Sasha for her apology, and then told her that she would be back to finish girl's night in a moment.

If I told her that I accepted her apology, then why do I feel the urge to knock her ass out, Amekia thought to herself as she made her way back to the living room.

Chapter Seven
Confrontation

Things at Carmen's job had been quiet, for the most part. The women who she caught gossiping about her stayed clear from her, and Mark didn't converse with her, unless he really had to. It had been two weeks since she filed her complaint, and she hadn't heard back from HR. The day was Wednesday, and the weather was starting to get colder as fall had come and winter was on its way. Carmen walked into the office fifteen minutes before she was to start her shift like she always did to at least drink some of her coffee and eat a yogurt of some sort. The break room was extra quiet, and no one occupied it. Even after the gossiping situation happened, they still would mingle in the break room, quietly. There was something off, but Carmen couldn't put her finger on it.

When the doors of the office were open, things were going smoothly, until there were older white men who walked in. She was in the hallway about to place a patient's chart on one of the doctor's desk when she saw them come in. She heard them ask for her, and she knew what they were there for. She scurried into the office, placed the chart on his desk, and left out of the room, only to walk right into the receptionist and the two men.

"Carmen, these men are here to see you," she stated, but her eyes held question. She was cool with Patricia.

"We'll take it from here. Is there a place we can talk to you in private?" The shorter of the two asked.

"Uh, yeah sure. Follow me right this way," Carmen responded. She knew they weren't police, but she couldn't help the sweat that dripped from her underarms. She escorted them into a vacant patient room and closed the door, noticing that all the doctors and nurses were watching her.

"Carmen, I'm Tom Weinstein, and this is Ronald Grimmick, and we are from Human Resources," the shorter of the two spoke.

"Hello," she said, and shook their hands.

"A couple of weeks ago, you filed a complaint against several people here. We just wanted to follow up and ask a few questions to you and the people that are involved."

"Sure."

They opened their briefcases and looked over Carmen's complaint. They asked her questions about the incident leading up to her filing the complaint. She explained the conversation that she overheard, and let the men know that she was never involved with Mark sexually, and that they only worked together. When she was done speaking with the two, she felt like a weight was lifted off her shoulders. When she opened the door, one of the nurses that was involved with the situation looked at Carmen with an icy look and kept walking, as if she was just passing by. Carmen knew that she was ear hustling, but decided to drop the situation. Carmen went back to work as usual, and throughout the day, everyone who was involved was pulled in to speak with Tom and Ronald. The stares that she received were all types of different shades of dirty.

Tom and Ronald left around two in the afternoon, and that was when everyone decided to blow up on Carmen. Each one taking their turn to tell her how they truly felt. For the second time, she was rendered speechless, but only because when the gentlemen left, she had hit record on her phone and caught everything that was said. It came from only the women, of course. Mark was smart enough to stay clear of Carmen.

It was six o' clock when Carmen was done and heading to her car. The day had been long and all she wanted to do was go home and drink herself to sleep. After the men had left, Carmen spoke to Patricia, and explained what was going on. She was informed that before Carmen had become a nurse there, the same thing happened to another nurse. But instead of filing a complaint, the nurse just packed up her things and left. The thing with those women was that they were territorial and wanted Mark for themselves, or even had sexual relations with him, but he never showed interest in them besides wanting to have sex with them. They didn't care if you weren't interested in him, they just knew that they had to do what they could when they figured he was showing interest in you.

When Carmen climbed into her car, there was a piece of paper on her windshield. She hadn't noticed it before. Looking around the parking lot, she didn't notice anything out of place, so she opened her door wide enough to stick her arm out and grab the paper, and slammed the door shut. The note on the paper read: *You fucked up!* It was written in red ink and was the only words on the page. She knew it had to be from someone from her office and she was going to save it to go along with the investigation. She drove home with the day's events on her mind.

***

The next morning, Carmen woke up with a hangover that left her with a banging headache and throwing up. She managed to get herself together and went to work. Day two of the mess that was going on, there was another note on her car that she didn't bother to read. She headed to work on a mission. She arrived her fifteen minutes early and headed straight for the break room, where everyone had congregated.

"Which one of you funky dog headed bitches keep leaving notes on my car?" She asked as soon as the door shut behind her.

The room grew quiet as all the women in the room looked at her like she was crazy. There was sass and smirks on their faces, and of course, Carmen knew that they wouldn't admit it. Ebony, the nurse who was ear hustling the day before, stood in front of them as if she was the leader of the group. She said, "How do you know that it's one of us? It could be from any-one."

"I know it's one of y'all. Every one of y'all are mad that," she paused mid-sentence, deciding against actually saying what she thought. Then she continued, "You know what, y'all got that. Just know that by placing notes on my windshield is only digging shit deeper," Carmen seethed through her teeth.

"You have no proof that either of us have done what you are accusing us of," Ebony stated matter-of-factly.

Carmen looked at Ebony and said, "And none of y'all have proof that I had any sexual relations with Mark. Yet y'all sit in this office and spread rumors saying that I did."

Ebony knew that Carmen was right, so she did nothing other than shut her mouth and went back to the group of women. Carmen looked at each of them, and if looks could kill, they would've fallen to the ground right at that moment. Carmen grabbed her things and headed to Mark's office. She opened his door without knocking, and she stood with her hands on her hips.

"Mark, those women in that break room are making it im-possible to be around. I have been working at this office for quite a while now, and I've managed to stay out of drama for the most part. Now that there is something going on around here, I'm being attacked. And I find that to be unfair. I'm tak-ing today off because I'm not going to work with people who are not only antagonizing me, but leaving me notes on my car," Carmen stated, fired up.

Mark looked at Carmen from his desk and contemplated what he was going to say. Removing his feet from the desk, he said, "I'm glad you came in here. I want to apologize for what has happened. I was insensitive to what you said. I don't know what is going on now, but I apologize for that, too. Go ahead and take the day off, and I will do my best to make sure I handle this situation."

"Make sure you tell them to stop leaving notes on my car. I don't have proof on who did it, but I know it was one of them. They also made time out of their day to leave a note on my car at my home, too. Let me get another one, and human resources will be the least of this office's problems."

"I will take care of it and look into it Carmen. I'm sorry you are dealing with this."

Carmen looked at Mark and rolled her eyes as she left out of his office. He wasn't sorry, he was just sorry that he was now in this position. Carmen made her way to her car, and yet again, there was another note on her windshield. She grabbed it and opened it as she climbed into her car. This note said: *After this is done, you're gonna wish that you killed yourself instead!* Her mouth dropped opened and she wondered if she should take the note inside and confront them.

Deciding against it, she started her car just as a *ding* sounded from her phone. Looking at the screen, it was a message from an unknown number that simply told her to kill herself. Dropping her phone into the passenger seat, she put her car into drive and shook her head. She knew soon enough that HR wasn't going to be able to do anything with these people, and she was going to take matters further.

Mimi

Chapter Eight
Something New

Ever since Jade had met Mr. Dixon, her mind had been on him, and no matter what she did, she couldn't shake it. Winter was approaching, and she decided that helping him and his son could be something that she could do, being that the holidays were coming up, so that there wouldn't be any strain between them.

The high school was buzzing with students lined up in the halls, making it to their first period, when she entered her office. On her desk was her normal case files, new ones, and a bouquet of pink and lavender roses surrounded with baby's breath, in a vase. Taking her coat and scarf off, she made her way to her desk, picked up the vase, and smelled the roses. A smile crept across her face as she plucked the card from off the card holder. It was from Mr. Dixon, of course, and it simply said for her to call him, with his phone number. *I wonder if he's thinking about me the way that I've been thinking about him.* She shook that thought from her head as she placed the case on top of her filing cabinet. She had work to do and vowed that she wouldn't allow those flowers, or Mr. Dixon, to invade her thoughts.

Several hours later, Jade looked at the clock and noticed that it was almost lunch time. She pulled out her phone and placed an order through Door Dash for some Mexican food, and continued to work. Her attention was brought to the flowers and she decided that there wouldn't be any harm with calling the man. What kind of woman would she be if she didn't at least thank him?

"Hello." His strong baritone voice rocked in her ear drum.

"Hello, Mr. Dixon, this is-" Jade started, but he cut her off.

"You can call me Darion, and I know who this is. I've been anticipating your call," he stated.

"Oh really?"

"Hell yeah. Why do you think I sent those flowers?" He asked with a slight chuckle.

"Well I thought you sent them because you are a nice person."

"That too. But I knew if I sent you flowers, I knew that you wouldn't be able to pass up the chance to call me and tell me thank you."

Jade blushed at his words. He was a little cocky, but nonetheless, he was right. She said, "Now what if I didn't call? What if I was a mean bitch that didn't care about some damn flowers, and never called?"

"From the day that I met you, I knew that you weren't that type. But for shits and giggles, let's say you were a mean bitch. If I didn't receive a call from you, I would have come up there, threw you over my shoulder caveman style, and dragged you to have lunch with me."

"So, you'd risk going to jail on a kidnapping charge just to take me to lunch?" Jade asked, walking over to her window, which didn't provide much of a view.

Darion paused before he responded. He said, "If it was my only shot to get you out on a date, then yes, I would."

Jade chuckled. She said, "I'm getting off at five today. Would you like to meet somewhere, let's say around seven-thirty?"

"Seven-thirty would be great. Where do you want to meet?"

"We could meet at the Northway Mall at The Cheesecake Factory."

With a grin on both of their faces, they agreed and hung up. The rest of Jade's workday went by with a breeze as she thought about her date. This was her first date that she'd had in a long time, and she couldn't have been more excited.

When five o' clock came, she climbed into her car and rushed home. Dropping her things at the door, she rushed to jump in the shower and wash with her favorite Dove Mango Butter body wash. When she exited the bathroom, she stood in front of her closet and tried to find something to wear. She decided on a white, V-neck, long sleeve, off the shoulder Maxi pencil sweater dress and black, pointy toed, strappy heels. She slipped two silver thick bangles on her wrist, placed a thick silver necklace on, and finished her look with square diamond earrings. Jade placed her hair in a high ponytail, and checked herself out in her full-length mirror. Satisfied with her look, she took a quick picture to post on her social media for later, and grabbed her things to leave.

As she pulled into the parking lot, her phone rang. It was Carmen calling her. She had some time to spare, so she answered, "Hey, skank."

"Fuck you. What you doing?" Carmen asked.

"Sitting in front of The Cheesecake Factory."

"For what? Don't you cook every damn night like you feed a husband and six kids?" Carmen asked with laughter.

Laughing, Jade responded, "I do not cook a lot."

"But that doesn't answer my question. What are you doing in front of The Cheesecake Factory?"

"If you must know, nosy, I'm getting ready to go on a date."

Carmen gasped at the shocking news. She said, "What? Not Jade? Who is the lucky person to win a date with Jade?"

Jade scanned the front of the Mall and noticed Darion standing out front, looking dapper, and holding a bouquet of flowers like the ones he sent her at work. He was wearing fitted black slacks, a black peacoat was over his crispy white button up shirt, and he wore black dress shoes. He must have had a fresh hair cut that day because his lineup was sharp as hell. Her pussy got moist just looking at him. She saw him look down at his watch, causing her attention to shift to Carmen, who was screaming *hello* on the other end of the phone.

"I'll tell you later. But I gotta go right now," Jade responded, and ended the call. She reached into the passenger seat and grabbed her waist length leather jacket and purse, and made her way out of the car. Jade, with an extra sway in her hips, made her way to where Darion was standing and stood in front of him. He eyed her from head to toe as a smile crept onto his face.

"You looking for me?" She asked, matching his smile.

"Damn. And I thought you couldn't get any finer in your work suit. Thank you, Jesus," Darion exaggerated.

"Thank you. You clean up nice yourself."

"These are for you," he spoke as he handed her the bouquet of flowers.

She held them, placing them to her nose and smelling the fragrance. She thanked him as they walked into the restaurant. They were seated promptly, and handed menus.

"Can I start you guys off with a drink?" The waitress asked cheerfully.

"Would you like something, beautiful?" Darion asked.

Jade looked at the drinks menu and decided on something nonalcoholic. She responded, "Yes, I'll take a Passion Mint Fizz."

"And I'll have a Corona," Darion said. The waitress smiled as she left, and they continued to look over the menu.

"How is Yajeel doing? He hasn't been to my office lately," Jade asked.

"He's doing well. He's slowly getting back to himself. He's joking more, smiling more, and it makes me happy to see him that way," Darion responded.

"I'm glad that he is. Do you still think that you need to have a therapy session?"

"I do think so. Just to be on the safe side."

"I'll work on that for you. But in the meantime, I would like to get to know you," Jade stated with a smile on her face.

They began to talk about any and everything that they could talk about. It was a breath of fresh air for both to be able to converse and listen to each other. When she spoke, he gave her the respect of shutting his mouth and listening, and she did the same for him. When the waitress came back to get their meal order, Jade ordered Jamaican black pepper shrimp that was served with rice, black beans, plantains, and marinated pineapples. She had no shame. She was a thick girl who liked to eat. Darion ordered the Carne Asada Steak, which came with white rice, fresh corn, and creamy ranchero sauce.

With their food in front of them, they continued with the conversation, and enjoyed their night. It was nine o' clock when they realized that the time flew by, and they'd both had a good time. Darion walked Jade to her car and wrapped his arms around her in a hug.

"Thank you. I really enjoyed myself tonight. It was a long time coming," Jade said, engulfing his cologne.

"It was my pleasure. I would like it if we could do this again," Darion responded.

"Just give me a call and I will see what I can manage. Just never on a Saturday."

"Why not?"

"It's girls' night, and we have been doing it for so many years that I wouldn't feel right ditching my girls to go on a date."

"I understand that. I'll keep that in mind. Send me a text when you get home so that I can know that you made it safe."

Jade displayed all thirty-two of her teeth as she nodded her head. Darion moved in and placed her chin in between his thumb and index finger. His lips covered hers as two quick pecks turned into a full-on tongue assault. Jade felt weak in the knees, being a sucker for a good kisser. She was almost like putty in his hands. She broke the kiss first and put distance between them. Jade knew herself, and there was plenty of times where she gave it up too soon, and any prospect she had on a relationship would end. She had a good feeling about Darion, and she wanted to take it further this time around. And for that, she would take it slow.

"Thank you again for the lovely night. I'll text you." Jade responded. She couldn't help but to notice his dick was standing at attention, and he did nothing to hide it. She licked her lips and climbed inside of her car. All the way home, she had a smile on her face. She couldn't wait until Saturday came so she could tell her girls about this man that she had met. It was too early to tell, but she could feel it in her bones that this, whatever it was going to be, was going to be perfect.

Chapter Nine
Snooping

"Brandon, you mind watching the girls this weekend? It's Amekia's turn to host the girl's night, and my mama is unavailable," Sasha asked her husband. It was only Wednesday, but she needed to know now so that she could have enough time to find a sitter.

"I didn't have any plans, so yeah, we should be good. We could have movie night and get stupid off some candy and ice cream," Brandon chuckled.

Sasha chuckled and said, "No sir. You will not have them hyped up off all that sugar, then have me come home drunk having to deal with them."

"Damn, I thought my plan was foolproof."

"Yeah okay," Sasha fluffed her pillows to get comfortable. She had an early morning. She was going to be going to visit her client, Nasir, in jail, and she wanted to get enough sleep to be alert and ready.

Brandon had just gotten out of the shower and was placing shea butter moisturizer on his skin. Things at home, after the blow up, were copasetic. Sasha realized that she never had a reason to believe that he was cheating, so she didn't need to start now. Brandon tried to play hard when she apologized to him. For him, that wasn't enough because, in his mind, she shouldn't have thought that he was cheating in the first place.

Sasha sent the girls to her mother's, and came home and cooked his favorite meal of blackened salmon with creamy mashed potatoes, garlic asparagus, and for dessert was her. She sucked the skin off his dick that night. She drained him to the point that he went right to sleep ass naked on the couch. He forgave her then.

"Come here," Brandon commanded.

Sasha opened her eyes and looked at him standing there naked. She knew what he wanted, and she hated to deny him, but she had an early day ahead of her. She said, "Brandon, I can't tonight. I have to get up early in the morning."

"I know you do, which is why I won't keep you up long," Brandon stated. He grabbed his semi hard dick in his hand and slowly stroked himself. Sasha thought about it as she looked at the time on the clock. It was only ten-fifteen.

"Tomorrow night, babe," she said as she shut her eyes.

"Tomorrow night? I'm horny the fuck now, what is tomorrow gonna do?"

"Brandon, I really don't want to get into it with you right now."

"I am your husband and you're making it seem like fucking me is a chore," he retorted, raising his voice.

Sasha sat up in the bed and said, "Lower your voice, the girls are sleeping."

"I wouldn't have to be loud if you just give me what I want. I know what you got to do in the morning, but shit, I remember there was a time where you would stay up late as hell with me, busting all kind of nuts. And as of late, it seems like you are pushing me off to the side like I'm a part of a to-do list."

"Oh, stop with the dramatics. You act like I didn't just give you the best blow job of your life a couple of days ago. You know what, I don't have time to argue about this shit. I'm going the fuck to bed," Sasha stated angrily. She laid back in the bed and placed the covers back over her body.

"You want to accuse me of cheating, and you don't see why I would be if I was. Look how you dismiss having sex with me. And dammit, Sasha, I'm tired of being put on the back burner. Everything comes before me, and that's unfair.

As your husband, I should come first. Before your girls, before your job, before everything."

Sasha tried her hardest to try to ignore him. He was working her nerve, and she didn't want to have this kind of conversation with him before she went to bed. She wouldn't get proper rest knowing that this wouldn't be resolved. She threw the covers back and climbed out of the bed. She yelled, "You want to fuck? Fine. Let's get this shit done and over with."

Brandon stood with a look of disgust on his face as he watched Sasha take her clothes off. He said, "If this what I got to do to get it, then I don't want it. I'll be sleeping downstairs in the guest bedroom. When you feel like you can act like a wife and put your husband first, you know where to find me."

Brandon grabbed some clothes from out of the closet and made his way downstairs. Sasha was left standing there with her shirt off and her pants down around her ankles. After a few moments, she realized that she looked ridiculous, and put her clothes back on. Walking to her side of the bed, she turned her lamp off and laid down. Sasha rarely cried, but she felt like her marriage was at a fragile stage and there was nothing that was making it easy. They were constantly arguing and, if it wasn't about them having sex and neglecting his needs, it was about her going out with her friends.

The silence in the room was killing her and her throat was dry. She headed to the kitchen to get her something to drink. As she was leaving the kitchen, she had to pass by the guest bedroom, and she paused as she heard sounds coming from the room. She stood quietly as she tried her hardest to hear what was going on. Light moans were coming from the room, and she recognized them as Brandon's. She figured that he was watching porn, so she continued her trek back upstairs.

The next morning, despite tossing and turning all night, Sasha got up and managed to be in a good mood. She crept around the house as to not wake up Brandon and the girls. It was five in the morning. They didn't need to be up until seven to get ready for school. By that time, she would be gone and at Albany County Jail. Making her cup of coffee to go, she hurried to the garage and left.

Within a half hour, she was at her destination and was getting searched. This was one of the perks of being an attorney. She was able to get inside of the jail before the visits for that day started, and she would be gone even before the visits would start. This was her first official meeting with Nasir, and she couldn't wait to hear his count firsthand. After she was searched, she was escorted to a room, which had a single picnic style table, and took a seat.

She was in the room for all of ten minutes when two guards walked in with a shackled Nasir. The orange jumpsuit that he wore was fitted, due to his bulging muscles. His hair was freshly cut, and his honey colored skin was glowing. His brown eyes penetrated Sasha as he looked her up and down, once he was fully in the room. The guards moved him to the opposite side of the table and sat him down, cuffing his wrists to the hook that was protruding from the table. The guards left out of the room, but stood guard at the door.

Sasha searched his eyes as he stared back at her and she had to admit to herself that this man was fine as hell. Just because she was married didn't mean that she couldn't look.

"Good morning, Mr. Franklin, my name is Mrs. Issacs. I am your new attorney. How are you doing?" Sasha stated and shook his hand.

"I am well, considering the position that I'm in," Nasir responded.

"I totally understand. Would you like to start from the beginning? I have read your file, but I'd like to hear it from the horse's mouth."

Nasir started from the beginning, reciting everything that was in the file. Sasha felt for him, but as his attorney, she couldn't show that shit. He was heartbroken behind what he saw, and from what she was hearing, she could get him out with some probation, and push come to shove, she could get him house arrest. When he was done telling his side, she let him know her plans of the crime of passion defense. She needed to know if he would protest if they were willing to give him probation or house arrest.

"Ma'am despite all of the things these damn pigs say about me, I am a respectable business owner and I have businesses to tend to. I don't care about no house arrest or probation if I can be a free person. I know that you're getting paid for this, so make it do what it do. That's all I ask," Nasir stated.

"I can assure you that I can do this. Whether I'm getting paid well for you being my client or not, I don't like to lose, so if I need to put on boxing gloves, I will. Just who you are alone, they are going to try to keep you locked in here. Your court date is next week. I have a few more things that I have to look into, but I will see you there." Sasha said with a smile.

"Thank you. My last attorney was a dick, but I can tell that this is gonna be a beautiful client/attorney thing," Nasir responded with a smile of his own. His medium full lips, white teeth, and dimples almost knocked Sasha's stockings off.

Blushing, Sasha stood up and took his hand into hers and said, "See you in a week."

"With an ass like that, I'll be seeing you in my dreams," Nasir smirked with a wink of his eye. Sasha was about to knock on the door so the guards could let her out. The pit of her stomach felt like butterflies. She wouldn't admit it to anyone, though. She turned around and looked at Nasir, who sat back in his chair with a smirk on his face. She walked over to him with a smirk of her own and bent close to his ear.

"I am a married woman, and your attorney. Have some class and respect that, or I will make sure your life is a living hell in here for you. You see the brown skin guard with the fade, that's my cousin, and if I give him the word, whatever it is I ask him to do, he will do it. Now you may be a kingpin on the streets and get what you want out there, but that ain't gonna work with me. Keep that shit in the back of your mind and we'll be all good. You got that?" Sasha stated and moved away from him, only to see that there was a smirk on his face still. She made her way to the door and paused when he began speaking.

"Just because I'm caged in doesn't mean that I won't get what I want. I'll play fair, for now. Off the record, though, I see something I want, whether you're married or not. Are you happily married? Cause being married and happily married are two different things. I'll see you in court next week, Mrs. Issacs."

With laughter ringing out behind her, Sasha knocked on the door. When the guards opened the door, she rushed out as if she was in a hurry. Well she sort of was, she needed to stop the leak that was between her legs.

She went back to her office after the visit with Nasir. Upon arriving, she told her receptionist to hold her calls for about ten minutes. Her excuse was she wanted to get her files in order of importance by when they must show up to court. In all actuality, she wanted to grab her bullet and release the nut that she held back after her meeting with Nasir. Her day was smooth sailing from there.

When Sasha arrived home, the house was quiet. Usually the girls were running to meet her at the door. After taking her heels off at the door, she went into the kitchen to grab a bottle of water and ended up finding a note from Brandon. It stated that he took the girls out for dinner and that he would bring something back for her.

Might as well grab a bottle of wine, she thought as she went into the pantry. Reaching to the top shelf, her fingers grazed her emergency bottle of pink Stella Rosa. She grabbed a wine glass and made her way upstairs. Going inside of the master bathroom, she ran the water for a bath and went back inside of the room. Walking to the dresser she shared with her husband to grab some clothes, she heard a faint buzzing sound. Opening the drawers to her husband's side, she searched until she came across a small black track phone. Looking at the screen, just a phone number appeared just before the person who was calling hung up. Instantly she went into the text messages to see if there was anything in there to let her know who it was calling. There was nothing except for times. *Don't think too much into it. This could have to do with his job.* Quickly she placed the phone back where she'd found it, and went to go take her bath.

All night, even after the girls and Brandon had made it back, she tried to keep the secret phone out of her mind. Even as she had sex with Brandon, she couldn't help but to think about that damn phone. She couldn't help but to wish that she didn't hear that phone ringing and she didn't have to snoop. That night she went to bed with a heavy mind and an even heavier heart.

Mimi

Chapter Ten
Surprise!

"I'm sorry, but what did you just say to me?" Amekia asked. It was the day before it was her turn to host girl's night, and she had gone to get a checkup with her gynecologist. She wasn't having symptoms for anything, but the way Donnie was acting had her thinking that he was dipping in somebody else's pot. She had called him the other day and his phone had just rang. She wasn't expecting what her doctor had just told her.

"It must be a shock for you because you told me that you just recently had your period. But Amekia, you are pregnant. Let me get the nurse in here so that she can get you set up for an ultrasound to see how far along you are," Dr. Black stated.

Amekia had been seeing Dr. Black since she was in her early twenties. She'd never steered Amekia wrong and Amekia didn't want to feel like she was doing so now. To hear that she was pregnant wasn't what she expected to hear. She sat on the paper covered table as her mind wandered. How the hell was she going to tell Donnie? Was she ready to be someone's mother? *Bitch, you should have been using condoms with this nigga. Now look at your dumb ass, pregnant with a married man's baby,* she mentally screamed at herself.

Five minutes later a nurse came into the room, dragging an ultrasound machine behind her. She held a warm smile on her face while she introduced herself and began to prep the machine. She instructed Amekia to open her makeshift gown and warned that the gel she was going to place on her stomach was going to be cold. Amekia was nervous because this was her reality, and she wanted to disappear. She closed her eyes as she felt the cold gel squirt on her stomach, and then the probe. The sound of a strong heartbeat made Amekia open her eyes. She looked at the screen and was confused at the black and white screen.

"This right here is your uterus, and this mass right here is the baby. Heartbeat is strong. Let me move this around a little bit and I will let you know just how far along you are." Nurse Niles smiled. Amekia was still in shock and tears welled in her eyes as she listened to her child's heartbeat.

"Can you tell what it is yet?" She asked.

"Not yet. Determining the size of the fetus, you are only about eleven weeks. We can tell as early as fourteen weeks, but it's not always accurate. We like to wait until you're between eighteen and twenty-one weeks. I'm just going to take a few more snaps and then you will be ready to go. Make sure that you stop at the front desk to schedule your next appointment. Just give me a few moments and I will have Dr. Black prescribe you some prenatal pills," the nurse stated.

"What if I want to get an abortion?" Amekia didn't know why she asked that. Just hearing the baby's heartbeat confirmed that she was keeping it.

"Well if that's what you decide to do, then contact the local Planned Parenthood and set an appointment. If that's what you want to do, then you need to act fast."

The tears cascaded down Amekia's face, and Nurse Niles soothingly rubbed her back. She pulled Amekia into a hug. Amekia managed to speak. She said, "I don't want an abortion. This was just unexpected, and I don't know how to feel about it. I should have been more careful, but I can't turn back the hands of time now."

"Just know that God is with you and that things only get better. Just remember to always pray and keep your faith."

"Thank you," Amekia simply said with a small smile on her face.

"Anytime, sweetheart. Let me go grab your prescriptions and then you can be on your way." Nurse Niles patted the top of Amekia's hands and exited the room. This was the easy part for Amekia, telling Donnie would be the hard part. Nurse Niles came back into the room with the prescriptions and let Amekia know to make her next appoint for three weeks out.

Amekia left the doctor's office with a heavy heart. There was no way that she was going back to work. She called her office and let the head dentist know that she wouldn't be in for the remainder of the day. She headed straight home and sat on her couch, lost in her thoughts. Amekia picked up her phone and gave Donnie a call.

"What's up?" He answered.

"Can you talk?" She asked with a sniffle.

"Not now. Are you okay?"

"No, but can you stop by my house when you get off?"

There was a pause on Donnie's end of the line. Moments later, he replied, "Sure. I get off at nine, though. Is it important?"

"Yes. But it can wait until you get off."

"Okay. I'll see you around nine-thirty."

Amekia hung the phone up and decided to go take a nap, wondering if she should tell her girls now or later.

***

Amekia's eyes sprung open as she heard banging. It was so loud she heard it in her sleep. Sitting up in her bed, she looked out the window and saw that she had slept longer than she'd intended to. It was dark outside, and as she looked at her phone to see what time it was, she knew that it was Donnie banging on the door. *Where the fuck is his key?* She thought.

"Alright, dammit, I'm coming," she yelled, making a bee-line for the door. She opened the door for Donnie and then ran to the bathroom. Her bladder was full and she needed to release it before she embarrassed herself and peed.

"What took you so long? I was out there for fifteen minutes, banging," Donnie stated as he sat on her bed and removed his shoes.

"I was knocked out, and my phone was still on vibrate from work," she answered, washing her hands.

Donnie laid back on the bed and motioned for Amekia to climb on top of him. She obliged and could instantly feel his hard dick pressing against her pussy. While she wanted nothing more than to ride his dick in that moment, she knew that she needed to tell him that she was pregnant. There was no doubt in her mind that he would flip. Shit, he might just even end things with her when she told him that she was going to keep it.

"What was so important that you wanted me to come over?" Donnie asked, getting straight to the point. His hands were on her waist as he guided her into grinding on his dick for a little dry humping.

"Well, I went to the doctor today," she stated. He stopped moving her and looked at her with wide curious eyes.

"For what?"

"Just for a checkup. I needed to make sure that I don't have anything."

"What you trying to say?" He asked as he sat up and leaned back onto his elbows. He said, "You think I've been fucking somebody else?"

"Umm, you forget that you're married, you are fucking somebody else. You need to just be fucking her. But that's beside the point. Point is, if you can cheat on her with me, then you can definitely stick your dick in somebody else just as easy."

"If you wanted to know if I was, all you had to do was ask."

"And not get a straight answer?"

"You went and got checked and still don't have an answer. All because you think that I would have an STD to show that I'm fucking somebody else. And I know you ain't got nothing because I've barely been fucking you or the woman I married. What's up with that anyway? I miss your pussy squeezing my dick. Why don't we get the important shit out the way so that I could slide up in you?" Donnie stated laying back down. As an afterthought he removed Amekia from his lap, took his dick out, slid her shorts to the side, and just let her pussy slide up and down his dick.

"I will tell you if you'd keep…your…dick…in…oh shit," Amekia moaned. This was not going the way that she had planned. Granted, she had been feigning for him to put it on her, but this was why she was pregnant now. Her pussy was leaking juices like she was holding a waterfall between her legs.

"You want me to put it in, or can you concentrate with the head rubbing against your clit?" Donnie had the nerve to ask as he guided his penis between her slit.

"I need to get off of you. That's how I'm gonna concentrate," she stated as she moved to climb off of him.

Donnie held her in place, dipping his head in her hole. Amekia threw her head back, and when he slid his whole dick inside of her, she wrapped her arms around the back of his neck and planted her feet. If he wanted to go for a ride, she was going to do just that. She squeezed her pussy muscles and bounced on top of him. Using his hand, he pulled her shirt and bra up, revealing her titties, and placed a nipple into his mouth.

He swirled his tongue around her nipple, causing Amekia to moan out as she bounced on him harder. She felt herself getting ready to cum.

"Mmm, babe, I'm about to cum. Get up so I don't nut inside you," Donnie whispered in ear, huskily.

She ignored him and continued to bounce. She felt his thigh muscles tighten, indicating he was ready to release. She bounced faster and harder, rocking her hips in a swopping motion, knowing that move alone would drive him crazy.

"Dammit, Amekia. I told you to move and now…oh fuck. I'm cumming," he stated as Amekia felt his dick jumping and leaking all his seeds inside her. Donnie leaned back onto the bed and watched Amekia rock back and forth on his semi hard penis. He looked at her like he was ready to knock her head from her shoulders.

"Why you looking at me like you want to fight?" Amekia said sweetly. She lifted her ass up enough for his penis to slip from inside of her. She remained sitting on his lap.

"Because you heard me telling you to move. You trying to trap a nigga or something?" He said angrily.

"Boy, bye. You are reaching, for one, and for two, it's too fucking late for me to trap you, if that's what you trying to call it," she retorted and climbed off of him.

"What the fuck you mean it's too late? You tryna tell me you pregnant?"

"I've been trying to tell you since you came in here. But as usual, your fucking dick couldn't stay in your pants long enough to listen."

Donnie sat up in the bed. He said, "I don't believe you. You just trying to use that so that I could leave my wife."

Amekia looked at him with bewilderment. Then she laughed. Was he serious? She went inside of her purse and grabbed the papers she had gotten from the doctor, along with the prenatal pills she had picked up. She said, "Nigga, I ain't never lied to you before. And as far as me wanting you to leave your wife, NOT. Never in these past three years did I ask for you to leave her. Nigga, I encouraged you to stay the fuck away from me and work on your marriage."

Donnie looked over the papers and he jumped from the bed. He yelled, "No! Fuck no! You not keeping this baby!"

Amekia, still laughing, said, "First of all, you don't tell me what to do with my body. I didn't act on this shit alone, and I'm definitely keeping my baby. OUR baby!"

"Amekia, please let's not do this. I don't need this ruining my marriage."

"Again, boy, bye. You weren't worried about your marriage then, nor are you really worried about it now, or else you wouldn't have come over here with fucking me on your mind. Now, no one knows that I'm even fucking anyone. And I plan to keep the father of my child a secret. I won't put you on child support, and the baby will hold my last name. We knew what we were doing from the beginning, Donnie."

Donnie sat at the edge of the bed with his hands on his head in deep thought. What the fuck was he going to do with a love child? What if his wife found out? She was gonna divorce him, take him for everything that he had, and he knew that his wife would give him a hard time with seeing his kids. He spoke solemnly, "How could you make any kind of decisions like that and you haven't spoken to me about it? You are forcing me to want to take care of a child that shouldn't even be considered being brought into this world."

"Whether you take care of this baby or not, he or she will be here in about seven months. I don't care if you're there or not. My baby will be taken care of accordingly."

Donnie stood up from his seat on the bed. He threw the papers onto the bed and looked at Amekia with sad eyes. He said, "Then I have no choice but to tell you that what we had is over."

"Okayyy. We were only fuck buddies, nothing more. But let me tell you this, when your wife starts nagging you, when she continues to withhold sex from you, or when she not sucking your dick the way that I do, don't come the fuck running back. You know your wife ain't a freak like me. When will she let you fuck her nasty then skeet on her face? Huh? Nigga, I bet you she doesn't let you fuck her in the throat. And you know I know that she doesn't do that shit because I do all that shit for you. Enjoy your vanilla styled sex life. And leave my key on the kitchen table on your way out," Amekia yelled behind him.

He regretted telling Amekia that his wife didn't fuck him the way that he desired. The deed was done, and the only thing that he could do was keep his word by staying away from Amekia.

Chapter Eleven
Life or Death

For the first time in the history of girl's night, it was cancelled. It was Amekia's turn to host it and she called all her girls to tell them that she was cancelling because she wasn't feeling well. She told them she thought she had a contagious stomach bug. But Carmen knew better than to believe that. Something was up with her friend, and come hell or high water, she was going to figure out what was up with her friend. She would give her some time, though.

Carmen had some things to take care of herself. The notes kept getting worse, and at this point, her glove compartment was filled with them. She constantly told Mark about them, but he did nothing to fix it. She needed to be away from that environment, and using her vacation time would be best for her at this moment. Bypassing Mark, she went straight to HR to see if she could use up her time. Keeping her fingers crossed, she prayed that they allowed it.

Work that day, Monday, had gone exceptionally well. And it seemed like everybody was walking on eggshells. The chatter during lunch time had ceased, and all was quiet. It was when she got home that she knew something was off. She noticed that her front window was broken. Her mother and sister were no longer there, and she was afraid someone might still be in there.

Cautiously, Carmen walked up the three stairs that led to her front door. The door was still locked, so she quickly unlocked and opened the door. As soon as she was inside, she grabbed the metal bat that she kept by the door and walked around her home as quietly as she could. Checking her back door, she noticed that it was still locked and everything in her house was still there. No missing laptop, desktop, or TVs. Walking toward the window that was broken, she noticed there was a brick laying on the ground with a piece of paper taped around it. She carefully picked it up, took the note off the brick, and read it. It said: *Just kill yourself now before it gets worse. You would be better off dead, anyway, so save the world some trouble and off yourself.*

The tears cascaded down her face. How could people be so cruel? This was a form of bullying that you only read about, instead of having it being done to you. Especially as an adult. Carmen always prided herself at being a strong woman, but this shit that had been going on at the office had put a lot of weight on her shoulders, and she could no longer bear it. What if it was true about the world being a better place without her?

Swiping her tears, she went into her backyard and found an old piece of wood that she was going to use for her garden. She used that to put on the window and went in search for the strongest liquor that she had. She found a bottle of Spirytus way in the back of her cabinet. Without another thought, Carmen guzzled a good amount of the alcohol, until the burn in her throat and chest egged her to stop.

Carmen just wanted to feel numbness. She cried the hardest that she had cried in years. Her mind wasn't clear and all she kept thinking about was the note, and all the ones that came before it. Then she blacked out. One minute she was sitting on her couch, and then the next minute, she was walking across the Craig Street Bridge. The highway was down below, and without a clear thought in her mind, she climbed over the rail. Her tears were nonstop as she watched the cars zooming under her. The words from that last note resonating through her head.

"Hey," a voice called out. Footsteps slapped the ground as she took one last look at the cars, and just as she made the decision to jump, she was grabbed by her arm and fell to the ground.

"Argh," she yelled. The feel of her knees and arms being scraped woke her from her slumber.

"What in the fuck is wrong with you?" The voice yelled. Carmen laid on the ground, looking up at the woman who stood over her.

"Huh?" Carmen asked, feeling disoriented.

"Where do you live? Do you need an ambulance?"

"No. And-and I li-live, oh my head."

"Come on, sit up and lean against the gate. Let me go grab my car and I will bring you home," the woman stated, and walked off.

Carmen's vision was coming back to her and she realized where she was. She lived a few blocks away on Howard Street, but how she had gotten to that bridge was a mystery to her. The woman climbed out of her car and walked back to Carmen.

"What's your name?" She asked, helping Carmen from the ground, and helping her into the car.

"Carmen."

"Okay, Carmen, I need you to tell me where you live."

"On Howard. I don't remember how I got here."

"It doesn't matter how you got here. What matters is that you tried to take your life. I'm quite sure that whatever is troubling you isn't worth it."

"My head is killing me. What time is it?"

"It's going on midnight."

The car got silent until they reached the corner of Howard and Main Avenue. Carmen gave her the directions, and a minute later, they pulled up to Carmen's house. The woman turned to Carmen and said, "My name is Denise. You want to talk about what has you down and ready to take your life?"

"I really don't. I just want to go inside and lay down."

"Okay. At least let me help you, and make sure that you are good."

"Sure," Carmen mumbled. Her mind was becoming un-foggy, and looking at her window, she remembered exactly why she was drinking the strongest bottle of liquor she could find. She was still drunk from the damage she put on that bottle, but she was able to think clearly.

After climbing out of the car, they made it inside of Carmen's house. Her house was torn up. There was broken glass everywhere, and furniture tossed around. She put her head down in shame as she looked at the mess. She knew she had done this because flashes of her doing it played back in her mind.

"Maybe we should call the police. To make a report," Denise stated.

"No need. I did this."

Carmen began to pick things up and Denise followed suit. Carmen just wanted to be alone, but she didn't want to be rude. She turned to Denise, who was in her own world, and watched her clean her mess up. Denise was small in height, maybe five foot even, and that was pushing it. Her skin was the color of caramelized sugar, and she had the smallest set of dimples known to humankind. She was dressed in black leggings, a white t-shirt, UGG boots, a Nike hoodie, and an infinity scarf.

"You don't have to help me. It's late, and I did this on my own," Carmen stated after grabbing the broom from the kitchen.

Denise stood up and placed her hand on her hip. She responded, "My mother committed suicide when I was just a little girl. Several years ago, I tried to commit suicide as well, and the same thing that I did for you, someone did for me. The person who saved me told me that everybody needs some-body, whether we want to admit it or not. We may be strangers but there is no way I'm going to leave you alone right now. I don't know what happened to make you want to take your life, but I'm going to stay and help you. Even if you don't want to talk about it."

Carmen didn't know what to say. Instead she continued to clean up, with the help of Denise. It was almost two in the morning when they got done. Carmen was still suffering from a headache when they finished, and she just wanted her bed. Thinking back to what happened, she decided to hand in her resignation and find a job elsewhere. This problem with har-assment was taking a toll on her mental health, and she had never felt so weak in her life. That job wasn't worth it. She was going to drop the harassment complaint and move on.

"Do you still have a headache?" Denise asked sitting on the sofa next to Carmen.

"If you can call a million tiny men using jack hammers in my head a headache, then yes," she chuckled.

"I got a remedy that will help. Do you have any tea and essential oils?"

"I should. Let me check in the bathroom," Carmen stated and began to get up off the couch.

"No. You stay right there, and I'll find it. You've had enough to deal with. Plus, I don't mind," Denise said with a smirk on her face. Carmen looked at Denise with a raised eye-brow and didn't say another word. Denise made her way to the bathroom to hunt down the essential oil. Carmen heard her moving things around in the kitchen one minute, and in the next, she saw blackness.

"Carmen. Here. Drink this right quick and then you can go back to sleep," Denise said, waking Carmen up. Sitting up on the couch, she grabbed the warm cup of tea from Denise and began to sip. She finished it and laid back on the couch. Denise passed her a rag smelling of lavender. Carmen placed it on her forehead and welcomed the sleepiness.

"Before I pass out again, I just want to thank you. You didn't have to do anything that you have done, and I don't know what it is that I can do to repay you," Carmen spoke.

"You don't have to thank me. Thank God that he put me in the right place at the right time. You are a beautiful woman on the outside, and I am sure that you are beautiful on the inside. You don't come across people like us. I can see that you are tired, so I'm gonna head out of here. I'm going to leave my phone number so that you can text me when you get up. I just would like it if you could let me know that you are okay," Denise stated, and patted Carmen on her thigh.

"Thank you again. The door locks from the inside, if you don't mind locking it on your way out. I'll text you when I get up," Carmen stated drowsily.

With a smile on her face, knowing that she had done a good deed, Denise walked out of Carmen's place and headed to her own.

The last thought running through Carmen's mind was *'What a fucking night.'*

Chapter Twelve
Lay Down Your Burdens

"Amekia, how are you feeling?" Jade asked that following Tuesday. Thanksgiving was coming up the next week and Jade wanted to make sure that her best friend was well enough to join the festivities for, not only Thanksgiving, but the upcoming girl's night.

"Hey, girl. I'm good. It was just a stomach bug, and you and them other heffas irking my nerves making it seem like it was something much more."

Jade chuckled. "Bitch, I'm just checking. We have never cancelled a girl's night, ever. It was weird being home on a Saturday."

"Who you telling?" Amekia giggled. She continued, "But I will be at your house with bells on come Saturday. I need some girl time."

"Thank God," Jade replied with a chuckle.

Amekia cleared her throat and asked, "Have you spoken to Sasha? Last girls' night, it seemed like she was holding in anger, and took that shit out on me. Since that night, I haven't heard from her."

"I have. She does seem like there is something wrong with her. She hasn't openly said anything, though."

"Maybe it could be work stressing her out. You know that she took that case that made headlines everywhere. The pressure from that alone could drive a person crazy."

"Oh yeah, I totally forgot that she did that. I think this girl's night we need to let all our burdens down, and express to each other how we are feeling. It only takes one thing to make a person snap and lose their mind. I'll make sure that we have plenty of wine. Cause I know that we gonna need it."

"Sounds like a plan to me." Amekia stated.

With that, they said their goodbyes and hung up the phone. Jade knew there was something going on with her girls, and she was going to get down to the nitty gritty. Her phone rang, indicating an incoming phone call was coming through. Looking at the screen, a smile spread across her face as she noticed her new boo was calling her.

"Hello," she sang into the phone, on a high that she never knew that she could feel.

"Good afternoon, Sunshine. How is work going?" He asked.

"Work is work as usual. Nothing new going on around here."

"Don't I know it? I know you can't wait until next week. School gonna be out for a couple days due to the holiday. Do you have any plans?" Darion asked.

"Actually, I do," Jade responded. She twirled a pen between her fingers as she went back and forth with herself on whether she should tell him her traditional plans for Thanksgiving. Maybe he wanted to spend the holiday with her.

"Usually, a person continues with explaining their plans," Darion chuckled.

Jade joined him, and she said, "I'm sorry, I got lost with my thoughts. My best friend Sasha usually holds Thanksgiving at her house. "

"That sounds like a fun evening. I asked because I wanted to see if you would like to spend the holiday with me, but you have plans already," Darion mentioned with sadness in his voice.

Dammit, I knew he was gonna ask me that, Jade thought to herself. Jade and Darion had been on three dates in the last two weeks, and while this was still new and fresh, all Jade wanted to do was be around this man. They didn't know what they had, but they both knew that they liked it. They hadn't mentioned to Yajeel that they were seeing each other, and Jade wouldn't push, but she just knew that it would be soon with how fast their relationship was going.

"Well, why don't you and Yajeel come to Sasha's?" Jade stated as an afterthought.

There was a pause on Darion's end of the line until he said, "That sounds like it would be fun but I haven't told him that I'm seeing his social worker so I don't think that would be a good idea. Would you like to get up on Friday?"

"Sure, that sounds like a plan. I have work to catch up on. I'll hit you up when I get off."

"Sounds like a plan. Talk to you later, and have a good day, beautiful."

"You do the same," Jade responded, and hit the end button on her phone. She couldn't help but to feel excited.

***

Jade had bought a sandwich platter from Subway for herself and her girls, and set bottles of wine in ice buckets. Usually, she served liquor, but she needed something smoother so that she could set the mood. At eight o'clock Sasha arrived, followed by Amekia, and finally was Carmen. The rest of the girls were shocked that she had brought a new face, and they all wondered why. They watched Carmen as she introduced the female to them one by one. They weren't rude, but Denise felt the standoffishness that they exuded. She understood why and only had to accept it because she knew that she was the new face.

Jade placed the sandwich platter on the coffee table and poured each woman a glass of Arbor Mist mango strawberry Moscato. She took her seat and began to speak. "For the last few weeks, I've noticed a shift in everybody, and it seems like everybody is off. I know usually we sit around, drink, and talk shit, but tonight I would like it if everybody lay their burdens down and speak about what is bothering them. I didn't know that we were going to have a new face tonight, because if I did, then I would have held off. I don't want to postpone it because we are a sisterhood and we need to help one another."

Carmen eyed Jade because she knew she was being shady towards her, but all the same, she knew that she needed to let her best friends know the turmoil that she was going through. Carmen had yet to mention the excessive amount of hate texts and notes she had been receiving as of late, nor did she tell them about her attempt at suicide. She wondered if that would even be a good idea. Carmen knew her friends weren't judgmental, but that would be the only way that she would be able to explain why Denise was there.

"So, who wants to go first?" Sasha asked as she sipped from her wine glass. They all looked between each other, wondering who would be bold enough to speak.

For a long minute, no one said anything. Sasha decided to be the one to speak up first. She figured if she was first, then she wouldn't have to speak last. She said, "Well, I guess I will. I wish that I could say that this heavy weight on my shoulders is from work, but I wouldn't be being totally honest about it. My client had court and they are releasing him on bail, and we have a date for trail. I believe that Brandon is cheating on me."

The girls gasped at her revelation, and Carmen was the first to speak, "Oh no, babe. Why do you think that?"

"He's just being too sneaky for me. For the last two or three years, he's been coming in later and later each night. He's claiming that its work, but I don't believe that entirely. I also don't have proof that he is, and that's what's really bothering me. My gut is telling me one thing, but my mind is telling me another. Oh yeah, and I found a phone in his drawer that gives me no clues. Just that it's a separate phone that he uses to communicate with someone else. The only thing that was in there was texts back and forth with different times, as if he was meeting up with this person."

What Sasha admitted to, was a shock to the group. They didn't know what to say, yet wanted to beat Brandon's ass for making their friend feel the way that she did. Amekia said, "I'm sorry that you are going through that. What are you going to do?"

"Nothing. At least not until I have proof. I could accuse him until I'm blue in the face, but the fact that I haven't caught him in the act is what's stopping me. It wouldn't be healthy for my marriage if I keep accusing him. So, I let it be. But it will always be in the back of my mind that he's out here swinging dick to another bitch."

"We're all sorry that this is happening. But as soon as you find out who the bitch is, you know we are down to ride and slap that hoe up," Jade responded, causing laughter to erupt in the room.

With the room quiet, Carmen said, "I guess I can go next. I know y'all are wondering why Denise is here. I saw it all over y'all faces. You all know about the shit that happened with work. Well I quit. It was too much to have on my mind all the time. I don't know exactly who it was, but I was getting hate notes stuck to my car, talking about my harassment case with HR was going to fall through, and Mark was doing nothing to take control of the situation. The notes were getting worse by the day, and it was taking its toll on me. Last week, after I handed in my resignation letter, I came home to find another hate note, but this time someone had taped it to a brick and threw it through my window. I was scared. I may act tough, but I'm not superwoman, and this shit that I've been dealing with was weighting heavy on me.

"After I cleaned up the mess that was created, I sat and drank Spirytus. Most of it was straight, from what I do remember. One minute I was on the couch drinking and crying, and then the next I was being dragged from off the Craig Street Bridge to the ground. Denise was the one who pulled me off that bridge, and I owe her my life. At my weakest moment, I found a new friend in her."

With tears in her eyes, all her girls came over to her and hugged her. In that moment, they accepted Denise into their circle, and thanked her for being there for their friend. There was not a dry eye in the room as they comforted Carmen and told her everything would be okay. No one asked why she didn't call them, there would have been nothing that they could have done that night. They thanked God that Denise was there.

Jade and Amekia didn't want to speak after the two heartbreaking things were mentioned from their friends. Jade decided that once everyone had everything out in the open, she hoped that they could all get back to their regular girls' night.

"Anybody need a refill?" Jade asked as she swiped the tears from her eyes. Everyone lifted their glass, except for Amekia, who still had a full glass. Her heart was heavy with the news of her being pregnant. She knew that she wouldn't be able to keep the news from her friends for long.

Jade continued after she was done filling the glasses, "Okay, not saying that what Carmen and Sasha have shared isn't important, because it is. I just want to shift the conversation a little bit, just to lighten up the room a bit. Your girl done found herself a new man."

Of course, everyone was excited. Jade had been single for the longest. She had one-night stands, but for her to be in a relationship was exciting for all of them. Amekia asked, "Who is he?"

"He is one of the student's parents. I know that it could be a messy situation, but I'm really feeling him. We've been out a few times, but we have to mention it to his son. I don't think that we should mention it yet because we are enjoying each other."

"We are happy for you. Enjoy it as long as you can because who knows how his son is going to react when he finds out." That was Carmen.

"Girl, I know it. His son had come to my office one day after me and his father had a date, and my dumb ass almost slipped and mentioned it to him," Jade chuckled.

Amekia sat up in her seat as she was about to respond, but a rush of sickness overtook her, and she ran to the bathroom and made it to the toilet just in time. Everybody ran behind her and watched as she threw up everything that she had in her stomach.

Carmen said, "Bitch, don't tell me you still got the stomach bug because if I get sick, I will fight you."

Amekia grabbed some tissue and wiped her mouth. A sheen of sweat covered her forehead, and she leaned against the wall. She looked at the concerned looks that stared back at her and she began to cry. She said, "I'm pregnant."

"What?" They shrieked.

"I'm almost twelve weeks," she admitted.

Sasha asked, "Who's the father?"

"A one night stand I had."

Jade and Carmen walked into the bathroom to help her from the floor. They helped her into the living room as Sasha went to the kitchen to grab a bottle of water and some crackers. Jade asked, "Why are you crying?"

"I should have done better with protecting myself. I told him and he wasn't happy about it. I'm gonna keep it but I don't know how I'm going to deal with being a single parent."

Sasha said, "Babe, you got all of us here to help you with that. We are a family, and whatever it is that you need, we got you. You know that. Him, whoever that deadbeat is, not wanting the baby, is his loss. Your baby will be loved, no matter what. We got you girl."

Denise finally spoke, "Congratulations."

They all turned to her, forgetting that she was there, and they laughed. They laughed so hard that Amekia almost peed on herself. The remainder of the evening they got to know Denise. She wasn't as bad as they thought that she would be. Inviting a new person to the group was a breath of fresh air for them, and they welcomed her in with open arms.

Chapter Thirteen
New Beginnings

Carmen and Denise made it back to Carmen's house at almost three o'clock in the morning. Denise decided to spend the night at Carmen's house because it was closer than her own. They spilled into the house in giggles after Carmen almost slipped on the ice that coated the sidewalk. It had lightly snowed the previous day. The snow was gone, but it had gotten cold enough to layer the streets and sidewalks with ice. Carmen walked into the kitchen to grab them some water, making them a quick sandwich in order to soak up the wine they had consumed.

"How did you like my girl's? They weren't too hard on you, which was surprising. I thought they would have given you shit," Carmen said, passing Denise the water and a sandwich.

"Shit, I thought so, too. But they were cool. I don't think that tonight was a good night to bring me," Denise stated, biting into the sandwich.

"If I would have known what was on the agenda, I don't think I would have brought you. I am quite sure that Jade threw everyone for a loop. I'm glad that she did, though. I don't think I would have mentioned what happened a week ago if she didn't do it."

The room fell silent, and then Denise said, "Can I tell you something?"

"Of course. What's up?"

"I have a crush on someone. I want to tell them, but I don't know how they would feel about it."

"What could be the issue? I know that it's only been two weeks since I've known you, but what I know is that you have a good heart. You're beautiful, so I don't see why a man would want to turn you down. Just tell him."

Denise chuckled and said, "If only it was that easy. For one, he is a she. I like women, Carmen."

"Oooh," Carmen stated, while eyeing Denise. She asked, "Well wouldn't it be easier if you told her. You know, since y'all both are women."

"You would think. My dilemma is that I don't know if she is into women."

"Just ask her. The worse thing that she could say is no."

"You're right," Denise stated.

"I'm calling it a night. The guest room is all yours. Fresh sheets are on the bed when you get ready to hit the sack. Thank you again for saving me. I owe you my life." Carmen leaned in to give Denise a hug. Denise returned the hug and when they released, Carmen walked to her room to get ready for bed. She brushed her teeth to get the stale taste of wine out of her mouth and placed on her silk, comfy, pajama short set. She had just reached la-la land when she heard the slow creak of her room door being opened. Her heart pounded in her chest, thinking that it was someone coming to rob her. The thought flew from her mind when she heard the softness of Denise's voice.

"What's wrong, Denise?" Carmen asked as she sat up in the bed.

"Do you like women?" Denise whispered.

"Huh?" Carmen asked, confused. She said, "I didn't hear you."

Denise walked closer to Carmen's bed. She noticed that Denise was only in a shirt. She looked up at Denise and watched her as Denise asked her again, "I said do you like women?"

Carmen was confused until she realized that the crush Denise was talking about was none other than herself. Carmen's mouth dropped open. Denise took a seat on the bed, looking at Carmen and waiting for her to respond.

After the shock wore off, Carmen finally responded, "Um, Denise, I don't like women."

"You said that the worse that could be said was no. I'm sorry."

"Sorry for what? Shooting your shot? Nothing wrong with that. I'm glad that you did ask, instead of becoming pushy about it." Carmen looked at Denise with a warm smile on her face. Denise looked heartbroken but besides offering support, Carmen couldn't do anything.

Denise stood from the bed and apologized again. Carmen just chucked it up to them being drunk and went back to bed. Hopefully, it would be a different story in the morning.

The smell of bacon and coffee woke Carmen from her sleep. After brushing her teeth and washing her face, Carmen made her way to the kitchen. Denise was standing at the stove mixing cheese into grits. Carmen took a seat at the table and watched as Denise wiggled her hips to a tune that was in her head. Denise turned from the position at the stove and screamed when she saw Carmen sitting at the table.

"You scared the shit out of me," Denise yelled.

"Ha. I didn't know that you didn't hear me until I noticed that you continued to cook while I took my seat," Carmen said with laughter.

"You can't be doing that to people. Look, I hope that it's okay that I cooked breakfast. I just wanted to apologize again for last night. I was wrong."

Carmen sat at the table biting her lip. She had to admit that when Denise left the room, she did think about what she had said. She thought about all her failed relationships that she had with men and figured that she wouldn't be opposed to trying something new with a woman. Granted, she had never been with a woman, but she thought what would hurt with trying.

"You don't have to apologize. I should have been more open to listening to you last night. I should have explained to you that, although I have never been with a woman, I'm not opposed to trying. Hell, I've tried everything at least once sexually, and dating a woman wouldn't be so harmful," Carmen said.

"No, you don't have to do that," Denise stated. She didn't want to make Carmen feel uncomfortable, and she still wanted to be friends with Carmen.

"I know I don't have to. I want to. I need a little sunshine in my life after what I dealt with. You were there for me when I was at my lowest, and don't mistake it, that isn't why I'm making this decision."

Denise placed a plate of bacon, eggs, grits, and toast in front of Carmen, and sat down next to her. She felt nervous as she asked, "Are you sure you want to give this a try?"

"I am," Carmen stated. She was nervous as well, but she needed to sound confident in order to convince herself that this was what she wanted. Denise stood up from her seat and walked over to Carmen. She bent down, lowering her face to Carmen's as she noticed that Carmen was holding her breath. A slight smile appeared on Denise's face as she placed a small kiss on Carmen's lips.

"That wasn't so bad," Carmen stated.

A sly smirk appeared on Denise's face and she replied, "Oh, sweetheart. This is only the beginning."

Chapter Fourteen
Two Can Play

"I don't know how I can thank you Mrs. Issacs. You did your thing in that court room," Nasir complimented Sasha.

"Staying out of trouble until the trial date would be thanks enough. This was nothing. The real test is when we appear for trial," Sasha stated with a smile on her face. She took Nasir's hand in hers and shook it firmly. She was done with court for the day and decided that after she made it to the bathroom, she would head to the office and get some paperwork done.

The bathroom was quiet as she went into a stall and emptied her full bladder. She'd been in the court room for hours and was upset she had to hold her pee in for so long. As she was finishing up, the door to the bathroom opened, and then closed. Not thinking anything of it, she continued to smooth out her outfit until she heard the lock on the door being turned. Fear ached her body as she thought about how she was going to get out of that small bathroom, and safely to her family.

"Um...hello?" She questioned. She didn't get an answer, and thought that maybe she was just hearing things. She flushed the toilet and exited the stall, only to jump at the sight of Nasir leaning against the wall with a smirk on his face.

"Please don't-" Sasha whispered, fearing the worse.

Nasir's expression changed from the smirk to confusion. He asked, "Do you think that I'm here to hurt you? I could never."

"I'm confused. Why are you in here then?" Sasha was frozen in fear and just wanted out of the bathroom.

"I know how this may look, but I assure you that I am not going to hurt you. Remember when we had our first visit that

I told you whatever I wanted, I got, even if it was a married woman."

"Yes, I remember. How can you chase after a married woman after what happened with your wife?" Sasha asked, before she realized what came from her mouth. It was insensitive, but she couldn't stop the question from falling from her mouth.

Nasir stood with his hands in his pockets and looked as if he was contemplating the question that she had asked him. He said, "My wife did what she did because she was a whore. I feel so deeply for her that I didn't see who she really was until that day. I gave that woman any and everything she could ever possibly want, without a question asked, and she still couldn't keep her pussy to herself. You are nothing like her, and I can tell. You are unhappy in your marriage. I don't know what it is that your husband isn't doing, but it shows on your face."

Sasha caught herself standing with her mouth open. She walked over to the sink and turned it on to wash her hands. More for a distraction than to actually wash them. She took her time in responding. She said, "Well, I'm the one thing that you can't have. Whatever I'm going through in my marriage will not make me want to cheat. I love my husband, and I took vows that I take profoundly serious."

Nasir slowly walked over to Sasha and turned the sink off. She froze, anticipating what it was that he was about to do. Before she knew it, he had backed her into the wall and stood so close to her that she could smell the mint on his breath from the double mint gum he was chewing on. With his eyes on her, he placed his hands on her waist and got down on his knees. Her breath was caught in her throat, unmoving. Nasir took the helm of her skirt and raised it over her hips, just until it rested onto her waist. He used his index and middle finger to rub against the fabric of her panties.

"Stop," She whispered. She put no effort or authority behind it. Nasir looked up at her, and she avoided his glare.

Nasir grabbed a hold of her leg and threw it over his shoulder. *Girl, get yourself together. This isn't right and you know it.* She scolded herself. Her thoughts went to Brandon and she knew that this wasn't right. Thinking and knowing that her husband was cheating was two different things, and currently in their marriage, she had only thought that he was cheating. What would that make her if she continued to let Nasir do what he was about to do? A sheen of sweat covered her forehead as her thoughts ran rampant. Just as she was about to push him off of her, she felt Nasir move her panties to the side and felt his nose between her slit. He inhaled deeply, turned on by her fragrance.

"You smell so fucking good," Nasir whispered against her pussy. He used his free hand to rub his dick through his pants. His tongue slithered out of his mouth and licked her from her pussy hole to the tip of her clit, causing her to shudder.

"This isn't right," she whined. *But damn it feels so good,* she thought.

"It doesn't have to be right in order for it to feel good. Let me just make you cum and you can go about your business," he said as her brushed his lips ever so lightly on her clit.

Using his fingers, Nasir spread her lips apart and flicked his tongue across her clit, causing her body to immediately shake. She couldn't remember the last time Brandon had licked her like this. Almost immediately, she was cumming on Nasir's tongue, and all her morals went out of the window, along with her vows.

If she was going to allow this, then she might as well go all out. She grabbed the back of his head and grinded her hips, causing herself to cum back to back multiple times. When it was all said and done, she couldn't help but to feel guilty.

When Nasir removed himself from between her legs, she moved to the sink with her head down. A smirk was adorned on Nasir's face as he stood next to her. He said, "You taste sweet. What's done is done, sweetheart. There is no reason for you to hold your head down. You're a beautiful, strong woman, and if you need to get your pussy licked, then so be it. Hold your head up and own that shit. Things happen. I'll be in contact."

Nasir was so sure of himself. He placed a kiss on Sasha's forehead and began to walk toward the door.

She quickly turned to him and said, "No. Nasir, this cannot happen again. While in this moment, what you just did was amazing, and made me forget momentarily that I'm having marital issues. The fact of the matter is, I am married, and I love my husband dearly. This wouldn't be worth breaking up my family."

Nasir again smirked. He didn't want to say anything else. He knew that he was gonna have her again, but didn't want to gloat in her face. Women were never able to tell him no. He was just going to wait. With a simple nod of his head, Nasir unlocked the door and walked out.

Sasha looked at herself in the mirror and began to fix herself up. This was a mistake, and she needed to confess to her husband. She didn't want to have this weighing over her head. Rushing out of the bathroom, she had her phone plastered to her ear, letting the law firm know that she had a family emergency to get to. Her assistant was going to bring her case files to her house so that she could play catch up over the next two days that she had off. She hoped that what she was about to tell her husband wouldn't fuck up Thanksgiving.

When Sasha arrived home, she was surprised that Brandon's car was parked outside of the garage. He was supposed to be at work, just like she was. She had her reasons as to why she was home. She entered their home, leaving her car parked next to his, and walked around trying to find him. Since they'd had the argument a few weeks ago, Brandon was still sleeping in the guest room. That's where she found him, laying on the bed, with his phone pressed to his ear. She stood on the outside of the door, out of his view, and listened to his conversation. From what she got from his side of the conversation, he was frustrated with the person that he was talking to.

"We have plenty to talk about, and I'd rather do it in person. So, let's stop all the bullshit and act like grown people here. I will see you tonight at the same time," he stated, and hung up the phone.

Sasha was confused as to what she had heard, but she could tell that the other person on the line was a female. Sasha heard Brandon getting up and made a beeline for the kitchen. She stood at the sink with the water running as if she was going to grab a cup of water.

"Oh shit. Hey, babe, I didn't hear you come in," Brandon stated, walking into the kitchen. When she turned to face him, she tried to read his expression, but there was nothing there.

"I just walked in. My throat was a little dry, so I wanted some water before I came to find you. What are you doing home?" She asked, sipping from the glass of water.

"I wasn't feeling well. My stomach was doing something crazy," Brandon stated. Then he raised an eyebrow and looked at his wife. Something was off with her, and he wanted to know. He continued, "What are you doing home? I thought that you had court today."

"I did, and it ended about an hour and a half ago. I have to go back in two months for trial. I was going to go to the office, but changed my mind. I just wanted to get some rest."

Brandon moved closer to Sasha and looked in her eyes. Something was bothering his wife. There was a sadness there. He asked, "Are you okay?"

Sasha thought about what happened in the courthouse bathroom with Nasir. She wanted to tell him, but the conversation that she heard Brandon having when she walked in made her change her mind. She managed a smile, and said, "I'm okay, babe. Thank you for asking."

"The girls don't have to be home for another three hours. You want to join me in the bedroom. Maybe try for a boy?" Brandon asked with a smirk on his face. He grabbed her by the arm and tried to drag her towards the bedroom.

"Um…uh…let me take a shower first. I've been in court all day and want to get the stench off of me," she said adverting his eye contact.

"Hell no. I don't care what you smell like. It feels like I haven't felt the inside of you in so long. Let's go."

There was no point in fighting him. He dragged her upstairs where they proceeded to have sex. She felt ashamed that her mind was on Nasir instead of her husband. That's when she knew that this was going to be a problem.

The next day, Thanksgiving, Sasha woke up at four to make sure that she got her food started. While it was only going to be her family and her girlfriends, she cooked enough food to feed six families. She needed to keep busy to keep her mind off of Nasir. At eight o'clock on the dot, her girls came to help her with cooking. She was a nervous wreck and needed to speak with them for some advice. Thankfully, Brandon was still upstairs sleeping.

"I need some advice from y'all," Sasha blurted out in a whisper.

The girls stopped what they were doing and looked at Sasha like she was crazy for whispering. Amekia asked, "Bitch, what the fuck you whispering for?"

"Brandon is upstairs sleeping, and I don't want him to hear what we talking about," Sasha admitted.

"Oooh, what did you do?" Carmen asked, causing the girls to laugh.

"Can y'all be the smart women that I know that y'all can be, and shut the fuck up and listen?"

Jade cleared her throat and said, "Fine. But you can't expect for us to be that way if you got us here at the ass crack of dawn cooking."

"It's hardly the ass crack of dawn, and all you bitches work, so being up at this time shouldn't bother y'all. If you bitches keep acting the fuck up, I won't say shit," Sasha warned. She was growing tired of them being childish. She was serious, and she needed to know how to handle this sticky situation.

"Okay, okay. What's on your mind?" Amekia asked, going back to chopping the celery.

Sasha exhaled, wondering if this was the right thing to do. These were her girls and they wouldn't judge her. In fact, Amekia would probably celebrate the infidelity. Sasha began, "Remember Nasir Franklin? The guy who caught his wife cheating and he killed his wife and the dude she was sleeping with?"

"Yes," they said in unison.

"We had court yesterday and I was able to get him out on bail. After the case, he thanked me, yada, yada, and I left to use the bathroom. While I was in the stall, Nasir came inside the bathroom and locked the door."

All of the girls paused what they were doing. She had their attention now. Not that she didn't when she first started speaking, but this had just gotten juicy. Jade thought back to what she'd said, "What the fuck for? Did he put his hands on you?"

"Oh, he did," Sasha sighed as she thought back to what happened inside of the bathroom, angry with herself for allowing the thought to make her panties drip. Nasir was a master with his tongue, and she had thought several times out of the day about what his dick was about.

Her girls rushed over to her to make sure that she was okay. Carmen asked, "Where did he hit you? You know you can tell the police, right?"

"No, no, no. He didn't put his hands on me in that way."

"Well in what way?" Amekia asked.

"He ate me out," she admitted, and dropped her head to the floor, feeling ashamed. Not that it happened, but because she liked it.

"What?" They shrieked.

"Shh, keep y'all voices down. I am so ashamed that I allowed this to happen. Here I am accusing Brandon of cheating, and look at what the fuck I allowed to happen, not even knowing if he's doing it or not. I feel so stupid and fucked up behind this. I need to tell him."

Amekia rolled her eyes. She said, "Friend, no the fuck you don't. He shouldn't even have you out here feeling like you need to accuse him. Keep that shit to yourself. Besides, it ain't gonna be something that you continue. It's better to leave it unsaid and in that bathroom, where it happened."

"Amekia, it's easy for us to say that because none of us are married. That's not how marriage works, and I think that you should tell Brandon," Carmen stated.

"This could tear my marriage apart. What if he isn't doing anything?" Sasha was damn near in tears. She was torn between keeping the secret and telling her husband.

"You do what you think is going to be right," Carmen stated.

Before they could go further into detail about what Sasha should do, they heard footsteps running down the stairs. All conversation halted as they all said good morning to Sasha's daughters and Brandon. For the remainder of the day, they enjoyed Thanksgiving.

Mimi

Chapter Fifteen
New Year New You

New Year's Eve had rolled around faster than Carmen expected. She was just spending Thanksgiving with her girls at Sasha's house. She had been unemployed for almost three months, and she enjoyed it. But she knew that her savings were not going to get her extremely far, and she needed to start getting back into the groove of things. Her relationship with Denise was moving at a snail's pace, and she had yet to tell anyone about it. It wasn't that she was ashamed, she was afraid of the reactions that she was going to get. Her mother frowned up same sex relationships because she grew up in a time where that was an abomination. While she knew her mother loved her, if she found out she was dating a girl, her mother would surely disown her.

Carmen was lying in bed with her mind all over the place, while wondering what she was going to wear out for the night with her girl's. She planned to tell them tonight about her relationship, due to the kiss that Denise and she would share at the stroke of midnight. Denise came into the room dressed in navy blue boy shorts and a white wife beater. Carmen looked at her and couldn't help but to feel her pussy come alive. They had gotten close with one another to get to know each other, but they had yet to have sex. Denise wanted Carmen to feel comfortable. Knowing this was her first same sex relationship, she didn't want to put any pressure on her. Carmen, however, wanted to move things to the next level.

"What are you wearing tonight?" Denise asked Carmen, taking a seat on the bed.

"I was just thinking about it. I'm between my black catsuit and my emerald green off the shoulder sweater dress," Carmen stated, leaning on her elbow, resting her head into her hand.

"I think you should do the catsuit. I'm trying to see your booty all night." Denise laughed, causing Carmen to join in.

"I knew you would say that. I'm going to tell the girls about us tonight."

"Are you sure? You know you don't have to rush to do that, right?"

"I know. But they are gonna be watching like a hawk once the ball drop and we kiss."

"Ooh, you plan on kissing little ole me at midnight? How did I ever get so lucky?" Denise giggled, trying to sound like a southern belle.

"Stop playing. You know damn well you planned on doing the same thing tonight."

"If that's what you want, you know I will be holding your hand through it all."

Carmen sighed and said, "It's not them I'm concerned about. They won't judge me. It's my mama that's going to be tough to crack. She grew up in the times where it was frowned upon. My biggest fear is that she will cast me out like she didn't give birth to me."

"I could hold your hand for that, as well. But mothers love me, so I doubt that she will do that. Lay it on her slowly, and we can work on it together."

"Ugh, I didn't think that this was going to be too hard. Maybe tomorrow we can do it, you know, just to get it out the way."

"Whatever you want to do, babe, I'm down." Denise stated.

Carmen looked at Denise and raised an eyebrow. She asked, "Whatever I want?"

Denise looked at Carmen when she noticed the tone in Carmen's voice changed. She detected lust and knew what was coming next. With a nod of her head, Denise agreed. Carmen, unexperienced and nervous, crawled across the bed to where Denise was and placed a kiss on her lips. Denise leaned back into the pillows as Carmen repositioned herself between Denise's legs. Denise stopped kissing Carmen by saying, "Wait."

"What? What do you mean wait?" Carmen was confused and frustrated. Her slit was throbbing hard between her legs. Without another word, Denise slithered from under Carmen and took the position that Carmen was just in. Carmen's face flustered as she realized that Denise wanted to take the lead on this. She thanked God for that. She didn't know what the fuck she was doing, and didn't want to look like a fool.

"Just relax okay," Denise said.

Carmen nodded her head as Denise placed her lips on hers and slid her tongue in her mouth. Denise pressed her body against hers as they heavily breathed and grinded their bodies together. Denise pulled Carmen's shirt up, releasing Carmen's titties, which were free from the confines of a bra. Carmen bit her bottom lip, anticipating Denise's next move. Her nipples were hard and waiting. Denise admired Carmen's breast. This wasn't the first time that she'd seen them, but this day was special, and she wanted to remember every single detail. Denise lowered her head and circled Carmen's nipple with her tongue. She used one hand to slip into Carmen's panties and rubbed her fingers across her clit, causing Carmen's eyes to the roll to the back of her head as she moaned out in pleasure.

"Oh my God. Don't stop," Carmen moaned.

"If you don't want me to stop this, I could only imagine how you're going to respond when my tongue is flicking on your clit," Denise whispered in Carmen's ear huskily.

"Oh my," Carmen moaned again. For two hours, they allowed their bodies to get acquainted with one another, causing Carmen's face to fluster with ecstasy.

It was time for them to get ready for a night out at Club Exit. They were having a New Year's Eve event and Carmen couldn't wait to attend with her friends. Like Denise had suggested, Carmen wore her black, leather, zippered catsuit with rhinestone, ankle strap, open-toe chunky heels. She added a little bit of eye liner and lip gloss. Denise decided to match with her boo and wore black leather pants and the matching leather zippered shirt that stopped just above her belly button. While Carmen wore her hair up in a bun, Denise wore her hair bone straight. Checking themselves in the mirror, they grabbed their matching waist length faux mink jackets and headed out to their Uber, which had been patiently waiting for four minutes.

By the time they reached the club, the line was wrapped around the building and barely moving. Luckily for Carmen and Denise, Jade, Amekia, Sasha, and Brandon had gotten there first and were just a few spots from the front door. Of course, when the other clubgoers saw the two jumping out of the Uber and meeting up with their people, they had something to say. Others shouted that it wasn't fair, but the bouncers were close friends with Brandon, and they turned a blind eye.

"Oh, I didn't get the memo that we were supposed to dress alike for this occasion," Amekia smartly stated. She was only playing, and Carmen knew this, but she couldn't help but to come back with a smart remark.

"I didn't know that we were supposed to be out here partying with a pregnant belly. Bitch, if something happens to my niece, I'ma kick somebody ass, and yours," Carmen quipped. "I'm pregnant, not handicapped. I'm not drinking and, belly and all, I'm allowed to enjoy myself. I promise to sit all night and dance in my seat, mommy dearest," Amekia replied with her middle finger in the air. Everyone laughed, including people that were surrounding them.

"No, but for real, I got to tell y'all something, and I don't want to wait until we get in to tell y'all," Carmen said with seriousness in her tone.

They looked at her with concern written on their faces. With Carmen's recent suicide attempt, they hoped that everything was okay with their friend. Jade asked, "Babe, what's going on? You okay? Are you still getting those notes?"

"No. It's nothing like that. But since you brought that up, I haven't received anything as of late, but I saw Patricia at the grocery store and she told me that a few women who used to work there had mentioned to HR that they had filed complaints and were looking back into it. They arrested Mark on the spot for sexual harassment and he is awaiting trial. What I wanted to tell y'all was that Denise and I are a couple," Carmen stated.

She wanted to run and hide after she had let her secret out of the bag. She watched as her friends looked at each other and then burst into laughter. That wasn't the response she was expecting, and she felt embarrassed. How could they do that to her?

Amekia spoke up, "Chile, finally."

"What do you mean, finally?" Carmen huffed.

"We been knowing what was up," Jade laughed.

"What? How?"

"We didn't think anything of it when you brought her to girl's night that first time. But afterwards, we peeped how y'all would look at each other on the sly. We are glad that you finally admitted it because it was hard as hell trying to keep Amekia's mouth shut," Jade said.

"You bitches is so funky. I swear, I can't stand y'all sometimes," Carmen stated and moved to the door to get checked. She heard them laughing behind her and couldn't help but smile on the inside. She thought, *And this is why I love them!*

The DJ was spinning *Stir Fry* by the Migos as they walked into the club. The club wasn't packed just yet and Amekia spotted a seat off in the corner, where she planned to stay all night to live stream everybody else partying it up on Facebook. After the girls and Brandon gave Amekia their coats, they made a beeline for the bar and ordered drinks. Nobody could stay off the dance floor as the DJ played hit after hit until it was time for the countdown. The night ended perfectly, with no incidents. Carmen couldn't wait to get Denise home.

The next morning when Carmen woke up, she decided that she would take Denise over to her mother's house and "come out" to her. Everything in her body had hoped that her mother would accept her. She was a nervous wreck. Denise did all she could to calm her nerves, but Carmen couldn't contain herself. When they arrived at Ms. Broward house, Carmen's stomach began to hurt.

"Maybe I should wait?" Carmen said as they sat in the car.

"We could do that. Except somebody already came to the window, so I'm sure they are waiting for you to come knock. Look, I'm going to be here by your side, no matter what. We don't have to do this today," Denise said, rubbing her hand across Carmen's. Carmen knew she had to do it today because, if she left, she knew that her mother would call her and hound her until she showed back up again. Carmen looked at her mother's house and saw the curtain move.

"No, we can do this. Thank you for being here for me. I don't know what I would do if you weren't here."

"Anytime, baby. Now let's go get the bible thrown at us," Denise joked.

As they climbed out of the car, Carmen couldn't help but to laugh. Her mother may have grown up in a different time, but her mother was no bible thumper. They proceeded to walk up the porch stairs and, when they made it to the top, the door swung open and her mother stood there with a hand on her hip.

"What took you so long to get out of the car, girl? Get in this house," Ms. Broward stated, and held the door open wide enough for Carmen and Denise to enter.

"Thank you for stalking, mama. Where is Ashlyn and the kids?" Carmen asked.

"Thanks to Amekia for getting that girl a job, she found her own apartment, and I finally got me some peace and quiet in here. Who's this?"

Damn, straight to the point, Carmen thought. She said, "Ma, this is my friend Denise. You got something to eat?"

"Yeah, I made some smothered pork chops, mashed potatoes, and turnip greens last night. I had gotten used to cooking so much while Ashlyn and the kids were here, I made too much last night. Make sure you make a plate for Denise. It's nice to meet you, young lady. I'm glad this girl done went out and made a new friend. I got tired of seeing her with those hussies."

"Oh, mama, you love Jade and them. And just for that, I'm telling them what you called them."

"And you think by doing so they gonna kick my ass? Tuh. I may be old, but I'm from the old school, and each one of y'all I'll put over my knee and whip y'all like it was 1932. Come see me in the living room when you're done."

Carmen and Denise were in a fit of giggles as they listened to Ms. Broward carry on. Carmen began to heat them up some food and thanked God that her rumbling stomach had saved her to give her more time. While they ate, they spoke in hushed whispers so that Ms. Broward wouldn't hear them. Time was winding down, and facing her mother was becoming less and less appealing.

"Just get it over with. It's like pulling a Band-Aid off," Denise whispered. Carmen rolled her eyes because this was nothing like pulling a Band-Aid off.

"Okay fine. But when this is done, we are going to get ice cream, and I get to lay in bed for the rest of the day without you complaining."

"If only I can do some things to you while we are in the bed," she whispered as she watched Carmen make her way into the living room. Wanting to give them privacy, but still wanting to support, Denise stayed in the kitchen until she was needed.

Carmen walked into the living room and sat next to her mother. Ms. Broward put the TV on mute and turned to her daughter. She asked, "What's wrong, baby? I can tell that something is troubling you."

"I need to talk to you about something, mama, but I'm scared to," Carmen admitted.

"Are you pregnant?"

"Hell no, I mean, no, mama, I'm not pregnant."

"Then what's wrong?"

"A few months ago, I was dealing with some issues at work and they became too heavy for me to deal with. Not thinking with a clear mind, I almost committed suicide, and Denise stopped me."

"Oh, my Lord! Why didn't you call someone?"

"That was the furthest thing from my mind. Denise came out of nowhere like a superhero and dragged me from that bridge. I only had a few scrapes and bruises. We remained in touch with one another until-" Carmen paused as she felt sweat trickle down her back.

"Until what, baby? Talk to me," her mother urged.

"We decided to be in a relationship together. I know that you've grown up in different times than we have, but, mama, the world is changing, and same sex couples are being more accepted today than when you were growing up. I love you with everything in my soul, mama, and it would hurt me tremendously if I didn't have your acceptance," Carmen blurted out. She breathed a sigh of relief as she looked at her mother, waiting for her response. Carmen could see that the wheels in her mother's head were turning. The wait was more agonizing than actually wanting to tell her mother.

"Now why would you think that I wouldn't accept you? When I decided to become a mother to you and your sister, I vowed to myself that I would, no matter what, stand by your choices. Good or bad. But if you were wrong, I was going to make sure that I let you know. This world is cruel, baby, and my job is to protect you. Who am I to judge who you are dating? You are grown and this is your life to live because I've already lived mine. If Denise is who you want to be with, then I can accept that. You're my baby, and I love you," Ms. Broward stated, causing Carmen to finally breathe easy. Tears welled up in her eyes, finally feeling good about telling her mother. A weight was lifted from her shoulders.

"Thank you, mama. I have stressed myself out for months wanting to tell you. I thought you were going to outcast me."

"I could never," Ms. Broward stated with a smile on her face. She continued, "Denise get your ass in here."

"Mama," Carmen exclaimed.

"What? Just cause she new don't mean nothing. The same way I talk to Sasha and them, I'm going to speak to her. Shiiiiit…She going to be around, she might as well get used to it."

Denise walked into the living room with laughter and took a seat next to Carmen. She said, "Carmen, my mama talks to me the same way. I'm used to it."

"I got a question for you two."

Carmen and Denise looked at each other and then to Ms. Broward. In unison, they asked, "What's that?"

With a sly smirk on her face, Ms. Broward looked at them and asked, "So y'all be bumping coochies and shit?"

Carmen's eyes opened wide as she yelled, "Mama."

Denise was just as shocked, but found it comical. Ms. Broward threw her head back in laughter as both her daughter and her girlfriend laughed at her expense.

Chapter Sixteen
Playing Games

Rinnnng... Rinnnng... Rinnng

The sound of her house phone ringing off of the hook had Jade rushing to get inside. She wondered who it could be. No one ever called her house phone. Dropping her bags at the door, she rushed over to the table in the living room, where her cordless phone sat on its base. It stopped ringing. Looking at the screen, she noticed that it was a private call, and that it wasn't this person's first time trying to call. There were six missed calls from the private caller, and she wondered who the hell it could have been trying to contact her privately. Placing the phone back in its cradle, she went back to the door and grabbed her bags to put her groceries up.

Davion was coming over for dinner, and she was prepared to rock his world. They had been together for a few months but hadn't done the do yet. She was tired of having to rely on her toys. She was surprised that he hadn't pressed her for sex yet. Often, she would wonder if he had another piece of pussy that he was hitting up to get satisfied, but she quickly threw that thought out of the window. She didn't want to think that way so soon in her relationship.

When Jade was done putting her groceries away, she took out her pots and pans to start cooking the dinner. She knew how to throw down in the kitchen, and she couldn't wait for him to taste her cooking. She was making pan seared garlic butter steak, cheesy bacon quinoa (made like baked macaroni and cheese), sliced mushroom, peppers, and onions sautéed in butter. She was as happy as can be as she danced around her kitchen listening to music from the early 2000's.

While she let the quinoa cook in the oven, she went to hop in the shower and get dressed for the evening. She got dressed in a red, cut out front, long sleeved, bodycon dress that stopped at her knees, with her favorite pair of white, open-toe, wrap up, stiletto heels. She had gotten her hair done over the weekend in kinky twists, which she wore down. She looked damn good, but the real prize was what she was wearing underneath. She'd recently purchased a white eyelash lace bralette and pantie set that left little to the imagination. She poured herself a glass of wine and waited for the quinoa to be finished to begin fixing the plates.

Her phone began ringing again as she had gone to the kitchen to turn the oven on. Running into the living room, she finally caught the phone in mid ring. She answered, "Hello?"

The other line was silent, but she could tell that there was somewhere there. After she said hello a couple more times, she hung up. *Now who the hell would be playing on my phone?* She thought. She unplugged her house phone, knowing that if there was an emergency, whoever needed to, would call her on her cell phone. Quickly dismissing the thought, she went back to the kitchen to set the table. Her doorbell rang as she was putting the final touches and her heart began to race. She seen this man on so many occasions, and she couldn't help but to feel this way every single time. If a man did that to you, it was worth keeping him around. Before she walked to the door, she checked herself in the mirror, and then proceeded to head to the door.

"Hey," she bashfully said as she opened the door.

Darion's mouth dropped when she opened the door. He stood there dressed in jeans, a Northface coat, and black Timberland boots. He was holding a bouquet of roses and couldn't take his eyes off of her.

"Damn, you look good as fuck," he exclaimed, and handed Jade the flowers. She invited him in, and went to place her flowers in a vase.

"These are beautiful. Thank you," she called from the kitchen. When she got back to the living room, he had placed his coat in the closet, as he always would.

"You're beautiful, so I had to get something that would be just as beautiful."

"Do you want something to drink? I had a glass of wine a little while ago, but I have beer and the hard stuff."

"I'll drink what you had. It smells good in here. I didn't know that you were going to be cooking. I thought we were going to order out."

"What kind of women have you been dealing with? I don't cook every day, but I do know how to throw down in the kitchen, if need be."

"By the smell, I can tell," Darion chuckled.

Jade went back inside of the living room, holding a glass of wine for the both of them.

"Dinner is done, by the way. I wasn't sure if you wanted to have a few drinks first."

"Hell yeah, I want to eat. My stomach started doing back flips when I smelled the food that you cooked. We could enjoy this wine while we eat," Darion stated.

He grabbed Jade by the hand as he pulled her up from the couch. He wrapped his arms around her waist, placing soft kisses on her neck as they made their way into the kitchen. Jade had outdone herself, she had candles lit on the table, soft music playing in the background, and the dishes covered to contain the heat. As if they were in a restaurant, Darion pulled her seat out and helped her sit. He then went to the other side to take his place. Within moments, they were chowing down and making small talk, just to get through dinner.

"Have you told Yajeel about us yet?" Jade asked as she wiped her mouth clean with a napkin.

"No. Not yet. I don't think that it's important right now for him to know. With us losing his mom not too long ago, I don't think he would approve of his old man jumping headfirst with anyone. I will know when the right time will be, and I will make sure that you are there with me telling him."

"It's no pressure. I just don't want him to catch us by accident, ya know."

"I understand, babe. Let us enjoy what we have for right now and we can worry about everything else later. Did you happen to make dessert? I thought I smelled something sweet," Darion asked, changing the subject. He knew that he wasn't going to mention dating Jade to Yajeel. He would never tell Jade that, and he would keep prolonging the subject as much as he could.

"Actually, I do have dessert. Head on into the living room and I will bring it in there after I'm done with this kitchen. Feel free to watch some TV as well," Jade smirked slyly.

Darion went into the living room as Jade had suggested while she rushed to clean off the table and place their dishes inside of the dishwasher. Afterwards, she made a quick run upstairs to freshen up a bit and take her dress off, revealing her sexy under garments. She added sheer white thigh high stockings and made her way back to the living room. She snuck up behind him, sliding her hands down the front of his chest.

Swaying her hips, she walked around the couch and stood in front of him with her hands on her hips. A smile appeared on his face as he grabbed her hands and pulled her onto his lap. Darion buried his face in between her breasts, and inhaled her scent deeply. Jade could feel his dick growing in between her legs as he rubbed his arms up and down her back.

Smoothly, Darion unsnapped Jade's bra, spilling her perky 38C sized breasts into his face. Using his hands to massage them, he stuck his tongue out and gave her nipples pleasure. Jade threw her head back as she felt her pussy becoming wetter by the second. Darion slid his hand inside of her panties, teasing her clit.

"Mmm. That feels good," she stated as she moved her hips like she was riding his dick. Jade's body began to shake and she knew she was about to cum.

"Let me see what that mouth do, ma," Darion whispered in her ear.

Happy to oblige, Jade stood from Darion's lap and brought him up with her. She bit her bottom lip as she took his shirt off and placed kisses on his chest softly. Unbuttoning his pants, she pulled them down along with his boxers. Eye level with the prettiest dick she had ever seen, she glided her tongue around his shaft to get it moist. Opening her mouth, Jade began to slowly suck on him.

Darion enjoyed just the little bit she had done so far. It had been a long time since he had some great head. Jade slowly took him further in her mouth, allowing his dick to hit the back of her throat. Momentarily, she glanced at him and felt proud that she made this nigga's mouth drop. His dick touched the back of her throat as she moved her head back and forth slowly as if she was on top of him, riding.

"Mmm," Darion moaned. He placed his hand on the back of her head, pushing himself further into her mouth. Pausing for a second, she shook her head as if she was aggressively saying no, and he quickly pulled out of her mouth.

"What happen? You didn't like that?" she asked innocently.

"I did, but I had to catch myself. I almost came and I'm still trying to feel that pussy."

Understanding where he was coming from, Jade smiled and turned her back to him. Hooking her fingers to the top of her panties, she seductively pulled them down. Darion cocked his hand back and smacked her ass cheek, causing her to yelp out. Grabbing his penis, he moved closer to Jade and slid his dick inside of her.

"Wait. The condom, Darion." Jade said.

He ignored her. There was no way that he could give up the opportunity to feel her raw. Jade wanted to move away from him to get him to stop, but his strokes felt too good to do so. It had been months since she felt anything real inside of her. She would allow it this one time.

"Damn, you got some good pussy," Darion moaned out. Just as she felt herself getting wet and juicy, all of two minutes after his statement, she felt Darion pull himself out. Turning around to face Darion, she was disappointed to see that his dick was already on its way to going soft and his semen was leaking on her floor.

"Please don't tell me that you nutted in me," Jade questioned. Her stomach turned at the thought alone.

"No. At least I don't think I did," he responded with a smile on his face.

"Fuck you smiling for? You think this shit is funny? And what was that anyway?"

"Ma, it's not my fault that you got some bomb ass pussy."

Jade was truly flabbergasted. She had never experienced no shit like that, and was upset with herself even further for allowing him to go in her raw. Grabbing her panties and bra, she went to the bathroom to take a shower. *Wait until I tell my girls this shit.* She thought to herself. Jade quickly washed away any trace of Darion being inside of her and put on a t-shirt and sweatpants when she got out. Trudging back to the living room, Jade noticed that Darion had fallen asleep with his pants at his ankles. She walked over to him and roughly tapped him on his shoulder.

"Darion, get up," Jade said annoyed.

"Huh?" He responded, jumping up.

"What you getting ready to do because I'm getting ready to call it a night."

Darion lifted his head from the back of the couch, where it was resting, and asked, "What do you mean what I'm getting ready to do? I thought I was staying the night with you."

Jade eyed him like he had lost his mind. She rolled her eyes and placed her hands on his hips as she announced, "Well I'm ready to go to bed right now, and I just remembered that I have a meeting to go to in the morning."

Darion stood up from the couch while pulling his pants up. Just then, her doorbell rang, and Jade wondered who the hell it could be. It was almost ten at night and she wasn't expecting anyone. Just then, the thought of Carmen almost taking her life entered her mind, and she rushed to the door. When she opened the door, on the opposite side stood a short female with a scowl on her face.

"Yes? Can I help you?" Jade asked.

"My man is in there," she stated shortly.

"I'm sorry, love, I think you may have the wrong house."

"No. I got the right house. You see, I followed him, and then I lost him. I sat in my car, trying to call him, but he wouldn't answer. I decided to drive around the area and noticed his car in your driveway."

Jade peeked her head out of the door and looked at Darion's car in her driveway. Jade didn't want to believe that this was happening right now. Being the bigger person, and trying to hold off on being rude, she gave the woman a small smile and said, "Are you sure that it's his car? You know, a lot of people are driving Dodge Chargers."

"Oh, I'm sure. I checked his registration sticker before I came and rung your doorbell."

Jade couldn't believe what she just heard. Is this what females are doing now a days to keep track of their dudes. If so, this isn't what she wanted. She shook her head and responded, "If this is what I gotta do to keep a nigga, I don't want it."

Jade heard Darion walking up behind her and turned to face him. The scowl on her face paused him in his footsteps as he looked back and forth between the two women. Jade looked at the woman who was looking back at her with a smirk on her face. She said, "See, I told you my nigga was here. Now you ain't the first bitch I had to press behind my nigga, but you will be the last. Because I'll be damned if any of you bitches think that y'all can come in between us. Darion, I let you stray one too many times, enough is enough."

Jade placed her hands on her hips and said, "Let's make this shit clear, sweetheart. If I knew he was fucking with somebody, he wouldn't have even gotten to sniff my perfume. His two-pump stroke ain't shit to be getting worked up over, and trust, even if you wouldn't have rung my bell, he was still going back home to you tonight."

"Two pump stroke?" Darion questioned. He had some nerve. He knew the bullshit he just did.

"Yes, that's what I said," Jade stated.

Before she knew it, the woman in front of her took a swing at her, but missed her face just by centimeters. *I know this bitch not tryna fight me over this dude. Ain't no way.* Jade thought. Before she had time to process what happened, the woman swung again, clipping her chin.

Jade didn't physically fight over men, but she was no punk neither, and her mama taught her if you get swung on first, you better make sure that you get the last. All her morals went out the window as she stood in a fighting stance and swung a mean right hook, catching the woman off guard, causing her to stumble down the stairs. Jade was on her after that, throwing blows that connected to every part of her body.

"Who the fuck you think you are?" Jade questioned as she repeatedly punched her in the face. Jade felt Darion trying to pull her off his woman, but all she did was turn her fists in his direction, leaving him dazed with a two piece.

"I'm calling the police," the scorned woman yelled from the ground. She was moving away from Jade by pushing herself with her feet across the ground. At that point, Jade didn't care what happened after this. This woman came to her place of residence and fought her. She would be the one to go to jail, not her.

"Go ahead, bitch, you the one that's gonna leave in handcuffs," Jade yelled. Darion moved around Jade and helped the woman off the ground.

"Tanya, get up. You not calling the police on this woman," Darion stated.

"You gonna take up for that hoe?" she yelled.

"Tanya, you were the one who came to her house and started this mess. You always doing some shit."

"Keep your dick in your pants and I won't have to keep doing this shit. You know what, Darion, I'm fucking done. She can have your ass. I've invested too much shit in this relationship and all you do is drag me through the dirt. Bring me STD's and everything. I hate you," Tanya yelled as she got up from the ground and went to her car that was down the block.

Darion sighed and put his hands on his hips, shaking his head. "Jade, I'm sorry that happened," Darion started.

"Fuck you and your sorry. How dare you have a bitch and then try to do something with me. It's men like you that make women like Tanya be on some fuck shit with other women. Tanya was probably a good female and you constantly doing fuck shit to her. Her only way to feel like she has a place in your life is to stalk you and act like a nut. Let me tell you something, don't contact me," Jade said.

She shook her head in disgust and walked away from Darion. Her face was stinging, and she knew there was a few scratches on her face. Walking in her house, she went straight to the bathroom to look in the mirror. Fresh scratch marks adorned her face. Sucking her teeth, she went and got the first aid kit and nursed her scratches. If she was to ever see Darion again, she'd knock his head clean off his shoulders, right after she gave him a piece of her mind.

Chapter Seventeen
Second Thoughts

Sasha sat in front of her vanity, taking a good look at herself. Her olive colored skin laid smoothly on her bone structure, her deep brown eyes were almond shaped, and her natural lashes were one's females would kill to have. Her medium full lips sat in a pouty state and her lone dimple on her left cheek stood out, as she didn't need to smile for it to appear. Looking amongst the many make-up brushes that sat upon her vanity, she found the right brush to perfectly do her eyebrows. As she looked closely in the mirror, she noticed that her youngest daughter, Aliana, was sneaking up behind her to scare her. Sasha continued what she was doing as if she didn't notice her.

"Ahhhh," her daughter yelled, jumping out next to Sasha.

"Ahh. Oh my God, you scared me, Aliana," Sasha stated with her hand over her chest, acting as if Aliana did indeed scare her.

"I got you mommy," Aliana giggled.

"You sure did. What are you doing creeping up on your mother like that?"

"Daddy told me to come get you. He cooked dinner."

Sasha raised her eyebrow and asked, "Oh did he?"

"Yes, mommy, and it smells so good. You don't smell it?"

"I do, but I thought that he had ordered take out. Let me go downstairs."

Sasha was genuinely surprised. Brandon never cooked dinner. Sasha held onto her daughter's hand as they made their way downstairs and into the kitchen. Just as Aliana had stated, Brandon had the table set and there were covered dishes of food. She looked at Brandon, who was standing near the table with a smile on his face.

"Brandon, what is all of this?" Sasha asked.

"I made dinner for my favorite girls," he beamed. He began to uncover the dishes and revealed creamy bacon and cheese couscous (baked macaroni and cheese style), garlic parmesan oven roasted asparagus, and Cajun sliced chicken breasts. Sasha's mouth dropped open. She was impressed.

"You cooked this?"

"Yeah. You sound like you don't believe that I cooked it."

"We have been together for how long? And you have never once indicated that you knew how to cook, and this well for the matter."

"That's because, as my wife, you assume the duty to make dinner. However, I thought that I could do something special for a change and cook for my girls."

Sasha raised her brow and folded her arms across her chest. She couldn't believe what she'd just heard. She asked, "Did you just say it's my duty as your wife to cook dinner?"

"Yes."

"Did you grow up in the forties? Because from what I know, marriage is an equal partnership. It's not about who does what because they are the husband or the wife. If you knew how to cook, you could have taken the time out and done so several nights during our marriage. I cook, clean, take care of the girls, and so much more. You lift not one finger, except for to work, eat, sleep, and shit."

"Whoa. Why are you coming at me? All I wanted to do was something nice for you and the girls. You're messing this moment up," Brandon stated as he slammed the dish rag into the sink.

"You messed it up when you decided to let that slick shit fly out of your mouth."

Brandon sighed deeply. He knew he was wrong for saying what he said, but he would never admit it to her. He felt that if it came out of his mouth, then he more than likely meant it. He asked, "Can we just enjoy dinner with the girls? Watch a movie?"

Sasha had wanted this from Brandon for months. When Aliana came and got her, she was getting ready to go out. She was going to push back her plans to have dinner, but she was so livid with Brandon that she didn't want to look at him. Simply, she stated, "You can. Before Aliana came and got me, I was getting ready to go meet with Amekia. She's emotional with this pregnancy."

"You gonna diss your family to go hang out with your friends?"

"No. I'm dissing you. You really should watch what you say," Sasha stated and headed back to their room to finish getting ready. Brandon stood there with a scowl on his face as he called his daughters to have dinner.

When Sasha was done getting ready, she headed to the living room, gave her girls a kiss on the forehead, and headed out of the door. For once, she felt good about leaving. After an argument, she'd usually isolate herself in her bedroom, but not tonight. Attaching her Bluetooth from her phone to her car, she put on Spotify to listen to soft R&B until she reached her destination.

Knock. Knock. Knock.

Sasha held her breath as she waited for the door to open. Sasha thought about turning back and just going to hang out with her family, but decided it was too late. She was already at the door. She heard the locks becoming undone and then the door swung open.

"Hey. Sorry I'm a little late, I got into an argument with my husband," Sasha rushed to explain. She walked inside and stood with her hands folded in front of her.

"It's okay. I know how those things can get," Nasir responded. He stood with a smile on his face. When he sent Sasha the text a few days ago, he didn't think that he would be able to convince her to come see him. They had spoken a week before he was able to convince her to come see him. When she was running late, he figured that she had changed her mind about coming and right before she knocked on the hotel room door, he was getting ready to call her.

Sasha unzipped her coat, let it fall from her arms, and passed it to Nasir, whose hand was waiting to take it to hang it up. She looked around the suite, spotting the couch, she walked over to take a seat. She said, "It smells good in here."

"I took the liberty of ordering some noodle soup from Pho Queen. I got us both the same thing, Kaui Tiao Ruea, which is basically beef meatballs mixed with a bunch of shit and noodles," he responded with a chuckle as he went to grab the items from the bag and place them on the table.

"I've always wanted to try that place. Never gotten around to it, thank you."

"You're welcome." Nasir walked to where she sat and held his hand out for her to take. She accepted his hand and he walked her to the table. He pulled out her seat and she sat with a smile. Brandon didn't do little things like this for her anymore, so she made sure to appreciate this kind gesture. Nasir sat down with Sasha and they began to grub on the noodles. For the most part, Sasha was enjoying her time, but she couldn't help but to feel the knot that formed in her stomach. Brandon faintly entered and exited her mind, making her feel a little guilty. *I wouldn't be here if he didn't make me feel like he was cheating.* She reasoned with herself.

When they finished eating, she helped him cleaned up their mess and they moved to the couch where they made light conversation. Sasha asked, "You know that there can't be anything between us, right? I'm married and we are client and attorney."

"Who says that anyone has to know about us? As far as your husband goes, I checked his background and I doubt that I have anything to worry about if I decided to make you mine."

Sasha scrunched her face up and asked, "If you decide to make me yours?"

A smile formed on his face and he said, "Maybe I shouldn't have said that in that way. I'm going to make you mine. I didn't want to sound like a cocky bastard."

Sasha smiled and said, "It's just that right before I left to come here tonight, my husband basically said that it's my wifely duty to cook, clean, take care of the girls, and wait on him hand and foot."

"Some men think that way, sweetheart."

"Yeah, I see. But we are in the year 2019 and marriages are different now. I'm burnt out after I come home from work and then having to do everything while he galivants and do whatever it is that he wants to do, I'm sick of it. Don't you know that through all the years he has never cooked, and then out of the blue he cooks dinner tonight, which is why the argument started about my wifely duties? Ooh, I'm sorry. I'm sure that you don't want to hear about my marriage."

"Don't worry about it, sweetheart. I get where you are coming from. Well, sort of. I saw the same thing with my parents. My mother was full of life, and over the years, as she attended to wifely duties, the light in her eyes dimmed. Women never get credit for all the shit that they hold on their backs, and it's mostly men who tear them down."

Sasha felt tears filling the rim of her eyes, but she refused to let them fall. She didn't come for this. Hell, she didn't know what she was there for. Nasir made her feel comfortable. From what she knew, a woman in her situation, the male wouldn't want to hear the woman he was trying to make his complain about her man. As she told him the recent things that had been going on in her marriage, he let her talk. He was more than an ear for her. He gave her feedback, and was honest with her. He didn't need to lie or fake it. That wasn't his style.

"Come, let me give you a massage," Nasir suggested. Even though she had been there for the better part of two hours, he could tell that she was still second guessing herself and why she was there. He wanted Sasha to relax. She didn't need to be so tense around him, especially since he wasn't trying to bring any harm to her.

"Oh, you don't have to do that." She stated.

"I know I don't have to. I want to."

"Well excuse me."

Nasir chuckled and handed her a white, fluffy, soft robe and directed her to go into the bathroom to change. *What am I doing? I'm a married woman,* she scolded herself, looking at her wedding ring. The recent argument ringing in her ear, she slowly took her clothes off, leaving her in her bra and panties. Placing the robe on and tying it shut tightly, she walked back into the bedroom. Nasir had candles placed around the room, soft R&B music was playing from a Bluetooth speaker, and there was a tray on the dresser that held quite a few massaging oils.

"Take the robe off," Nasir stated.

"I'd rather just keep it around my waist with my top half exposed," Sasha stated firmly. Her back was to him because she just knew that if she were looking in his eyes, then she would have dropped her robe with no questions asked.

Nasir spoke again, "I asked you to take off your robe. Now I'm telling you to take it off. I'm not going to do anything that would hurt you, Sasha."

Taking a quick moment to think it over, she did not see any harm in a massage resulting her having to be just in her undergarments. She reasoned to herself that it only made sense because that's how it would be done inside of the salon. Sasha dropped her robe and bashfully climbed onto the king-sized bed. Sasha could not see, but Nasir had a smile on his face. He grabbed a bottle of Shea Moisture body oil and poured it into his hands. Climbing onto the bed with her, he began to work on her shoulders and work his way down. Soon enough, Sasha was relaxed and closed her eyes.

When she opened her eyes again, the room was completely dark. There was a blanket covering her, and Nasir laid next to her, still fully clothed. She looked at the time on the alarm clock that sat on the nightstand and was shocked to see that it was already one forty-six in the morning. She slid out of the bed and began to look for her clothes.

"Just stay until the morning," Nasir mumbled as he watched her through squinted eyes.

"I can't, Nasir, and you know that," she whispered to him.

"Ma, please. I just want to be able to hold you." There was something in Nasir's voice that she couldn't place, but it gave her pause in her movements. She knew that she would be pushing it. She had told Brandon that she was going to be with Amekia. She knew that he wouldn't call her, he couldn't stand her.

"I can only stay until five, Nasir, and then I have to go. I'm kicking myself for even coming." She threw her clothes back onto the chair, where they were.

Nasir moved to the edge of the bed and grabbed her hand. He pulled her to him and embraced her into a hug. He knew this was hard for her, but if she didn't have an ounce of attraction for him, he knew she wouldn't have answered his text, let alone come. Nasir pulled her onto the bed, and once she was laying down, he moved on top of her, looking at her in her eyes. He wanted nothing more than to feel her insides and feel her lips on his. So, he made his move. Without much resistance, he kissed her lips. Her body trembled as he slowly parted her lips with his tongue. He pressed his body against hers, leaning slightly to the left so he wouldn't crush her frame.

"I don't know if I can do this," she whispered, breaking the kiss. She moved her face away from his.

"Shh. Just let it happen," he whispered back as he kissed her from her ear to her neck.

"But-"

"No buts," he stated, and slid his hand up her thigh. Her skin was soft. Something about soft skin did something to Nasir and his dick was awakened within seconds. He found her lips again as his hand moved further up her inner thigh and rested on the lace fabric that was between him and her wetness. He groaned as he moved her panties to the side and slid his finger in her wetness. Her pussy was like a puddle. Sliding his finger over her clit, he watched her as her eyes tightly shut and she bit her bottom lip. She wanted to moan, but didn't want to give him the satisfaction. Nasir stopped abruptly, leaving Sasha in wonderment. She felt him remove himself from the bed and by the slither of light that shined inside of the room, she could tell that he was coming out of his clothes.

Sasha had every opportunity to run, instead she stayed. She was going to kick herself every day for this, but she convinced herself that it would be just this one time and she would pass his case to someone else so that she wouldn't have to see him. It would have been an easy fix, but what she didn't know, Nasir wasn't going to be that easy to get rid of.

Nasir made love to her body as if he was her husband and he had missed her. Her body molded to his in ways that his deceased wife didn't. After he made love to her, he made sure to fuck her, giving up all of the aggression that he was holding in. She clawed at him, bit him, and even slapped him at one point, but the fact of the matter was that she enjoyed it.

He feasted on her womanhood as if it were his last meal, even dipping his tongue in her ass. He had done the one thing that Brandon didn't do, and she didn't even have to ask him. Just once wouldn't be enough, at least she thought she wouldn't be seeing him again. She didn't leave the hotel room until well after six. She knew it was going to be an argument with Brandon, but she didn't care. She was on a high that nobody, not even her husband, was going to knock her off.

Mimi

Chapter Eighteen
Baby Daddy Drama

Amekia wanted nothing more than to have Donnie be a father to her child, but he wasn't budging. He stopped taking her calls and placed her on the block list. If she wasn't pregnant, she wouldn't have cared as much, but it seemed like, since she had gotten pregnant, all she had done was eat and cry. She was nearing her sixth month and her round belly stuck out as if she were having twins. Her daughter was active and kept her up at night, by flipping and kicking her ribs all night. She swore that she would be the best mother her daughter could have, and would make sure that she was all her daughter would need.

Amekia was lying in bed Saturday night, after girl's night. They had cut it short because Brandon had come around and started with Sasha about her not being a wife to him. She had told her girls about what happened the night that he cooked, so of course, when he brought that up, they verbally attacked him, causing Sasha to call it a night. It was becoming the norm lately, either he was constantly calling her to come home, or he was starting something while they were at their house. Amekia was going to go to the next one, but if Brandon was up to his fuckery, she wouldn't attend another one until Sasha got that shit in order.

"Girl, you ain't never lied. He's showing insecurities he's never shown before," Amekia stated to Carmen. They were chatting away on the phone about what happened at girl's night.

"If they are always arguing, how the hell is Sasha walking around glowing, periodically getting lost in her thoughts, and then smiling like she had some inside joke?" Amekia stated. She was the sober one, and she couldn't help but to notice everything about her friends. She didn't have on rose colored glasses, and she knew there was something up with Sasha, but to find out what it was, would be proven harder than what she thought.

"Maybe she's pregnant and doesn't want to tell us yet because she hasn't thought about keeping it. You know how hard her pregnancies were with the girls."

"I do know. And I also know that that smile she wears on her face ain't from a baby that she's not sure about keeping."

Carmen thought about what Amekia was saying and then gasped. She asked, "Do you think that she's cheating?"

"I sure hope that she is. After all, she thinks that Brandon is cheating, it wouldn't hurt to get her a little get back."

"But they are married," Carmen stated.

"We all know that, but sometimes, instead of hurting your spouse by telling them the truth about unhappiness, you go out and do the most hurtful thing in a marriage, and that's cheat. This is why I refuse to get married. I'd be in jail if my husband cheated on me."

"Didn't she say that she didn't have any proof that he was cheating?"

"Yeah."

"So, what if he's not cheating? Then she just out there opening her pocketbook to anybody and destroying her marriage."

Amekia now had grown tired of talking about her best friend and her marital problems. Quiet as it was kept, she was still salty about the comment that Sasha had made months ago about her not knowing what love was. Amekia was a tough cookie, but if there was one thing in the whole entire world that she could have, it would be love. Yes, she'd been in relationships and came close to an engagement, but none of the men genuinely loved her.

In her adult life, she had been with four men. The first one was David, she had met him at a bar, and it wasn't supposed to go further than a one-night stand. They ended up dating, but she found out nearing the end, he was just with her because she was a pretty face to have around for when his company would have parties and events.

Next was Leon, he was a patient of one of the dentists at her job. He offered to take her out, and from there, the relationship blossomed. He wined and dined her, made her feel like the only girl in the world, and she would have done anything for him, except do a jail bid. She didn't know him like she thought she did. He was arrested on robbery charges. How he was able to woo her was because he was a thief. When he called her from jail, asking her to post his bail, she quickly hung up and changed her number.

After dealing with Leon, she vowed that she was going to stay away from men. And that seemed to be true for a good year and a half, until she went to a Christmas party with Sasha for her firm. He was tall, brown skinned, and finer than wine. They instantly clicked and began dating. When they had been together for almost a year, Fazion admitted to her that he was thinking about asking her to marry him, but he had to come clean about some things and hoped that she would understand. She was confused about what it could have been. He told her that he was attracted to men, as well as women, and that at first, he was just using her to save face around his family, but he was getting older and had to be true to himself.

She was hurt. She had loved him with everything in her. He admitted to having sex with men unprotected, and she had to thank God that she always insisted on them using protection. If he was truthful from the beginning, then she would have considered still dealing with him. Ultimately, the lying is what made her step back from him. She wished him well and never wanted to see him again. Before she had gotten pregnant, she had run into him at the supermarket and couldn't believe how out of the closet he had become. He was transitioning to become a woman, and his lace front looked better on him than it would have on her.

Then there was Donnie. She loved him, but in a way that she hadn't loved the others. They were friends before anything, and she could share everything with him. The only thing between them was the fact that he didn't belong to her. He was another woman's husband, and she knew she would never have him to herself. Then she got pregnant.

She didn't want him to be hers, she just wanted him to be there for their child. She understood that he was married and that an outside child would break up his marriage, but they both knew what they were doing when they wouldn't use protection. They both knew what could possibly happen, but she was the only one paying for it. She had to carry a child and deal with her emotions all by herself, and it wasn't fair. It was cool if he didn't want to fuck with her, it didn't matter. It was the fact that he wasn't allowing their child to experience what his other children was experiencing, and that was having a father. Whether she knew or not that he wouldn't accept her child, it still wasn't fair.

"Girl, did you hear me?" Carmen said, catching Amekia's attention. She hadn't realized that she had checked out of their conversation.

"Oh no. I zoned out for a minute. It's been happening a lot lately."

"I said that I was going to go because Denise wants some loving."

"Ew. Keep that to yourself," Amekia responded, causing Carmen to laugh. They said their good-byes and hung up.

Amekia had to use the bathroom and as soon as her butt hit the toilet, somebody began ringing her doorbell in urgency. *Fuck whoever at that damn door. They gonna have to wait. I'm not rushing,* she thought to herself. After washing her hands, she finally made it to her door, looking out of the peephole. With her heart stuck in her throat, she opened the door.

"What do you want?" She asked with her arms folded across her chest.

"I needed to see you," Donnie said. He was leaning against the door frame, his eyes red. Amekia wanted to feel sorry for whatever he was going through, but the fact that he had dismissed her after telling him she was pregnant, she couldn't find the strength to feel sorry.

"See me for what? You made it truly clear that you didn't want to have anything to do with me," she stated, her face set in a scowl.

"Come on Amekia. I need to talk to you."

Amekia looked at him up and down, and the ice wall that she had set on her heart was slowly melting. Everything in her screamed for her to slam the door in his face. But the truth was that she did miss him. She missed the times where they would just sit around and talk about any and everything, laugh and joke, and even watch TV. Exhaling, she pushed the door open wider and let him in. He walked past her and headed into the living room, taking a seat on the couch. After she closed the door, she followed him, and sat on the chaise lounge that was on the opposite side of the room.

"Why are you sitting all the way over there?" Donnie asked.

"Why are you here? You said you needed to see me; you're seeing me. So, either you tell me what you want, or you can leave."

Donnie sighed. The last thing that he wanted was for her to have an attitude with him. He knew he was the reason why she was this way with him. He would never admit it, though. Donnie was as stubborn as a mule, and would never admit when he was wrong. The reason for his visit was because it had been eating him up inside for months about his baby. He wanted more than anything to be a father to her child, but the fact that she wasn't his wife was what made it hard.

If his wife found out that he was having a baby outside of their marriage, she would surely file for divorce. Despite him fucking with Amekia, he loved his wife, more than life itself. He cheated with Amekia because she was convenient for him. She made the time to see him, she made time for them to spend time together, to have sex. Whereas, with his wife, it seemed like he was being placed on a to-do list.

"I missed you," Donnie responded.

"I missed you, too, Donnie, but you don't see me calling you, or popping up at your house to tell you so. You left me out to dry."

"What did you want me to do? You know I would no longer be married of she found out that I'm having a baby outside of our marriage."

"Well it still may happen because I'm having this baby. You think you are the only one that was surprised at this pregnancy? That is not how it was supposed to go, but we both were playing around by not using protection."

"I know, Amekia. You must understand where I'm coming from, though. Do you know how hard this is going to be to explain?"

"Absolutely not. You know why? Because no one knows who my child's father is. All they know is that I had a one-night stand, and when I told him, he didn't want to have anything to do with me or the baby. So, trust, your secret is safe.

I want my daughter to have a chance at having a father, like your other kids do. You know, I didn't have a father growing up. I don't want that for my daughter, walking this earth without knowing her father. I had no choice in the matter. My father was killed, and I walked this earth looking for a man's love to fill that void. I don't want that for her when she has a living father. What if she gets older and starts asking about her father? What am I supposed to tell her? That she was the product of an affair with a married man and he didn't want to be her father because he was more concerned with what his wife was going to say? Because he feared a divorce? That ain't fair that you are determining her future without even being a part of her presence now, while she is still in the womb."

Donnie sat up in his seat and folded his hands. He said, "You don't have to tell her you had an affair."

"I won't lie to my child," Amekia said sternly. She continued, "Look, this isn't going anywhere, so I think you need to leave. This is stress that I don't need. However, if it means anything to you, my due date is May 16th."

"Amekia, please."

"Amekia please what? Cause you ain't saying much of nothing. I'm tired of this charade with you, Donnie. Either you're gonna be there or not."

"What about my wife and kids?"

"What about them? You weren't worried about them when you were fucking me. You weren't worried about them when you were here spending time with me."

"Why are you being so emotional about it? You say you understand but what you are asking me to do something that's going to have major consequences in the end for me."

"Donnie this isn't about you. Hell, it ain't even about me. You know what, get the fuck out. I'm not in the business of asking you repeatedly for you to be a father to my child. Fuck you. Get out," Amekia yelled. She picked up a pillow from off of her chaise and began to hit Donnie over the head with it.

He got up from his spot and headed to the door. This conversation went nowhere Donnie had hoped. He hoped that she would just drop him being a father to her child. In his mind, he knew that wasn't going to happen.

"Don't contact me when you go into labor," Donnie yelled like a bitch as he stormed out of the door.

Amekia slammed the door and hurriedly walked to her room. She climbed onto her bed and cuddled up into a ball. She cried into her pillow until her eyes were puffy, red, and sore. She vowed that she would never hit him up for anything. She was going to do her best at raising her child alone and to her that's all that mattered. *Fuck Donnie and his wife. They both can kiss my ass,* she thought to herself as she fell asleep with her hand on her belly.

Chapter Nineteen
Girls

Three days after the fight she had with Davion's woman, Jade had called an emergency girls meeting. It was rare that a girls meeting was called, but when it was, everyone knew that it was some type of an emergency.

Jade sent out a group text for her girls to meet her at Scarboroughs Restaurant in Latham. Girls' night was two days away, but Jade couldn't wait to tell her girls what happened. She arrived at the restaurant first, and decided to order a round of drinks for her friends. Amekia was first to arrive, and Jade knew something was up with her friend. Amekia was the type of female that you wouldn't catch without being glammed up. Today, she was dressed down, in jeans, sneakers, a pull over hoodie, and her hair was drawn back in a low ponytail. Jade raised her hand so Amekia could see her, and she watched as her friend made her way to her. When Amekia made it to Jade's table, Jade helped her into her seat and looked at Amekia in the face.

"Are you okay?" Jade asked. She was genuinely concerned about her friend. Amekia was almost six months pregnant, and the way she looked, was as if she was carrying the world on her shoulders.

"Yeah," Amekia responded with a weak smile. She sounded stuffy, like she had been crying. Her eyes were puffy, and she had a sadness in her eyes that anyone that didn't know her could tell.

"Are you sure?"

"Yes. You called this meeting. I don't want to make this about me."

"Amekia, you're pregnant, and whatever you're going through, you don't need to stress about."

"Jade, I promise, I'm fine," Amekia stated with a smile on her face. At that moment, Jade decided to leave it alone.

Carmen and Sasha waltzed in looking their bests. Jade looked at her girls, and something was off about Sasha. She had a glow to her face that only pregnant women carry, and Jade instantly thought that her friend was pregnant and hiding it. Carmen and Sasha approached the table, and gave hugs and kisses around the table. Amekia put a smile on her face and avoided as much eye contact as she could.

"Before I start, Sasha are you pregnant?" Jade asked, straight to the point.

"What?" Sasha shrieked, causing people to turn in the direction of their table.

"Bitch, you heard me. You out here glowing and shit, and the only explanation would be that you got a bun in your oven."

"Hell no, I'm not pregnant," Sasha replied with her lip twisted to the side. She took her coat off and placed it on the back of her seat.

"Mhm, how do you know?"

"Cause I'm on birth control, bitch. Now mind your business and tell us why the fuck you brought us here when we could be discussing this on Saturday."

Carmen, Amekia, and Jade looked at Sasha. Carmen spoke the question that they all wondered. She asked, "Why the fuck are you on birth control when you are married?"

Sasha exhaled. She wasn't going to tell her girls until Saturday, but since they were questioning her now, she might as well tell them. She said, "Brandon came home two months ago talking about he wanted another baby. I'm at the height of my career and don't need another child right now."

"Isn't that a bit selfish?" Amekia asked.

"No. Men don't have to deal with this shit like women do. My marriage isn't even strong enough to bring in another child right now. So, I decided to get on birth control to make sure that it didn't happen."

"Does Brandon know?" That was Amekia.

Sasha turned to Amekia and gave her, her full attention. She said, "What I do with my body doesn't concern him, whether he is my husband or not. If the shoe was on the other foot, I wouldn't doubt that he would start wearing condoms. And you know what, I would have to sit there and allow it. So, no, he doesn't know, and he doesn't need to know."

"Mmm," Amekia stated as she went back to grab her glass of water to sip from. She continued, "I thought marriage was about open communication."

"You aren't married so you wouldn't know shit about it. Do you have an issue with me, Amekia? Cause you've been making salty comments my way for the past couple of months," Sasha asked with a roll of her neck.

Amekia sat up in her seat and leaned on the table. She said, "Actually, I do have an issue with you. A few months ago, you made a smart ass comment about my hoe ass not knowing what love is."

"Are you kidding me? You took that shit serious. Didn't I apologize for that?"

"Apology or not, if I'm your friend, you don't say no shit like that. As a matter of fact, you are always saying slick shit to me, but don't say half of the shit that you say to me to Carmen or Jade. I should be asking if you have an issue with me."

"Hey," Jade yelled for their attention. She was getting tired of her two friends going at each other necks. There was an underlying issue that needed to be aired out between the two, but now was not the time.

"What the fuck is going on with y'all two? Y'all are friends and all y'all do is bicker like y'all got animosity between y'all," Carmen stated as she looked back and forth between Sasha and Amekia.

Sasha soothed her voice before she responded. There were people watching them and she didn't want them to get kicked out before anyone of them found out about why Jade had asked them there. She said, "I apologized for what I had said. She should have made it clear that she wasn't going to accept it. I say a lot of shit towards you, Amekia, because it always seems like you have something negative to say about my marriage."

"I don't say shit negative. I tell you the truth. I'm not going to apologize. I was taught, apology or not, if you say something from your mouth, then you thought about what was said and still said it, whether it hurts the person or not. So whatever hurtful shit you say, you had time to process it before it left your mouth."

"What about the shit you say to me? You don't think before you speak?"

"Of course, I do. But what I am saying is that you say hurtful shit."

"And you think what you say isn't hurtful?"

Amekia was done with the conversation, and was tired of having to repeat herself. She pushed her chair back, getting ready to leave. She said, "I didn't say it wasn't hurtful. I'm telling you it's the truth. And as the saying goes, the truth hurts. Jade, call me and let me know what it is that you wanted us to know. I'm outta here."

Jade stood up from her seat and called out to Amekia, "Come on, Amekia, don't be like that."

"Weren't you the one who told me I was pregnant and that I shouldn't have to stress? This environment is stressing me out."

Sasha butted in and said, "Let her leave. She has a more pressing issue with finding her baby's father than anybody else's issues."

Carmen and Jade's mouth hung open. Amekia paused in her footsteps, and turned around to look at Sasha. There were fresh tears in Amekia's eyes, and Jade and Carmen couldn't do anything to defuse the situation. Carmen looked at Sasha with an evil glare. She said, "Sasha, what is wrong with you?"

"She was the one who said the truth hurts," Sasha responded, while she plucked imaginary dirt from her fingers.

"I swear to God if I didn't consider you my friend and I wasn't pregnant, I'd be on your ass. You being my friend is what's letting you slide, yet again. You being my friend is what's stopping me from bursting your bubble. Fuck you, Sasha. And I mean that from the very bottom of my heart." With that, Amekia turned back around and walked out of the restaurant. The table was quiet. Carmen and Jade looked at Sasha with scowls on their faces as they took their seats.

"Are you gonna mention what you brought us here for, or can I go?" Sasha asked sipping from her cup.

"You can go. I don't know what is up with you, but lately you've been a bitch, and it's showing," Jade stated.

"Grow up, Jade. Amekia is the queen of dishing it out but not being able to take it. And frankly, I'm tired of the bullshit, and she can kiss my ass. Instead of worrying about what I do in my marriage, she need to find her baby's father. She ain't gonna know shit about taking care of that baby, and quite honestly, I don't think she's going to be able to handle it," Sasha stated, getting up from the table.

"Let me tell you something, Sasha, that is your friend that you are talking about. She's going through enough as it is and is terrified about raising this baby, and instead of being a bitch to her, you need to be helping her. You're the only one that has kids. You should be offering a helping hand instead of criticizing her."

Sasha knew Jade was right. She couldn't help but to feel bad about what had transpired. Sasha was surprised at herself, at how she acted, and knew that she would need to have a heart to heart with Amekia. Without a response, Sasha left the restaurant and made her way home, feeling less of a woman for putting her friend down. Remaining at the restaurant, Carmen and Jade decided to stay and order something to eat.

"What the fuck just happened?" Carmen asked, placing her hands on her forehead, confused.

"I don't know. I don't believe that I want to know."

"I guess you could tell me what the emergency was, since those two heffas don't know how to act."

"You are not going to believe it. Remember the dude I had told y'all about?"

"Yeah. What about him? I remember that you wanted to let his son know about y'all so it wouldn't be any confusion."

"That's the one. Anyway, I invited him over a couple of days ago for dinner and sex. Lots of sex, and boy was I disappointed. He gave me the two-pump stroke and had the nerve to ask me to stay the night. I haven't felt so disgusted in my life. Then afterwards, his girlfriend knocked on the door."

"Bitch, you lying," Carmen rebutted. She was in shock, but was intrigued. She asked, "What happened?"

"She tried to fight me. But I waxed that ass and kicked both of them from my house. I told that nigga to never come back my way." Jade giggled as she thought about that day. She was heated in the moment, but she was glad that she could laugh at it now.

"What is wrong with men? They went from chivalry and being a gentleman, to slobs and lazy, cheating bums. Where the men that our grandparents and their parents had? They wouldn't have cents to their name and still make sure that their family was taken care of. Look at Amekia. She's having her first child due to a one-night stand, and holding a lot on her shoulders. And one of her friends is shitting on her like single women don't do the damn thing when it comes to raising kids. The times in this world have changed, and it pisses me off," Carmen responded.

"The situation with Sasha is mind boggling. It's like she's changing into a different person, like she's becoming more outspoken. I like that she is, because she was as quiet as a church mouse, but she don't need to take her frustrations out on Amekia."

"I agree. Let's eat so I can take my ass home. It's safe to say that girl's night is cancelled?"

Jade nodded her head as she dug into her grilled steak and mashed potatoes. She vowed that she would do what she had to do in order to bring her friends together.

***

Jade hadn't made any progress with Sasha nor Amekia. Amekia had either turned her phone off, or disconnected it, or both, because Jade had gotten the voicemail for a few days, but here it was three weeks after the incident, and she was now getting a disconnected message. Jade made several attempts to stop at her house and her job, but she was neve at her job, and she refused to open the door. Jade was worried about her friend, and needed to make sure that she was okay.

Jade decided that enough was enough. She was going to go over to Amekia's house and find a way to break in. Desperate times had called for desperate measures, and she was desperate to make sure that her friend was okay. The night before she came up with this plan, she was feeling okay. The next morning, she woke up having the chills and a fever that was over a hundred and two degrees. She nursed herself all that day, and decided that she would try the next day, but she woke up with the same feeling. Worry rocked her body and, as much as she hated going to the emergency room, she made her way there. There was something wrong, and instead of her fever going away, it rose to 104.2. She couldn't shake the chills and hoped like hell they didn't tell her she had the flu.

When she arrived, there wasn't a lot of people, so she was able to get to the back faster than what she expected. The nurse took her vitals and immediately ordered something for her fever. She explained her symptoms to the nurse, and her nurse assured her that the doctor would be in soon. As soon as the nurse left, Jade wrapped herself in the hospital blanket and fell asleep.

"Ms. Rios, what's going on with you today?" The doctor asked when she walked in.

Jade rattled off what her symptoms were. The doctor checked her stomach, her heart, and lungs, and told Jade to sit tight. She was going to run a bunch of tests and told Jade to stay awake long enough for the nurse to come back and take some blood samples. Jade did what was asked of her, and once again when the nurse left, she fell right to sleep.

When she woke up, she still had the chills, but her fever was gone, and she was grateful for that. By this time she had been inside of the hospital for three hours and was growing hungry. She wanted more than anything to call one of her girls to bring her something to eat, but she wanted to wait until her test results had come back before she did so. Everything under the sun popped into Jade's head as to what could be wrong with her. The one thing she kept going back to was that she was having beginning symptoms to the flu. Jade had the flu when she was a child, and it was the worst thing that she had experienced. And what she was going through was what she remembered from her childhood.

Dr. Melbourne came in with her nurse with a grim look on her face. Jade began to shake and feared the worse. Dr. Melbourne took a seat on the bed next to Jade, looked into her eyes, and took her hand into hers.

Jade said, "I knew it was the flu. But you don't have to look so sad. I had it when I was younger and got through it, I'm fairly in good health, I'm sure I can get through it again."

"Do you have anyone here with you today?" Dr. Melbourne asked.

"No. I think I should be fine with driving myself home. I got here just fine," Jade chuckled.

"We ran a bunch of tests and we initially thought that it was the flu, but we ran STD tests, a pregnancy test, an HIV test -"

Jade stopped listening after what the doctor had said. It felt like there was ringing in her head that she couldn't get rid of and was blocking out her hearing. She didn't understand why they ran those tests for flu-like symptoms. Jade was in a daze and forty-five minutes later, she was walking to her car with a bunch of pamphlets and a request for her to follow up with her primary care physician.

How could this be happening? She drove straight home, and climbed into her bed, crying until her nose bled.

Mimi

Chapter Twenty
Feeling Thy Self

It was now March, and it had been two months since Sasha had spoken to, seen, or heard from her best friends. She expected Amekia not to talk to her, but was surprised when she didn't get an answer from Carmen and Jade. She called them for two weeks straight before she finally gave up and tried to get her head back into her marriage. Balancing work, home, and a side piece was starting to become a bit much for her.

The relationship between her and Nas was kept under wraps, due to Sasha being his attorney. She was putting her job at risk by seeing him. Sasha tried her darndest to stay away from Nas, but after the first night they spent together, she was hooked. It was like she was a crackhead and he was the crack. He bought her gifts, ate her pussy and ass, and took time to listen to her. These were all things that Brandon didn't do, which made it easier for Sasha to fall for Nas.

The gifts that she received from Nas were ones that she only saw celebrities wear. Her wardrobe grew extensively, causing Brandon to become a little suspicious. She would lie and say that she found the items at Goodwill. Every time she went to see Nas, she would feel guilty and vow that she would end things before she got too deep. She thought that she had a handle on things, but truth be told, she'd lost all control of the situation the first night she slept with him. Sasha didn't know that when the time was right, Nas was going to do everything in his power to make Sasha his.

Brandon felt that his marriage was on the brink of ending because there was something that changed in his wife that he couldn't pinpoint. He suspected that she had been cheating, but the only thing that he found when he went snooping was texts from her clients, and nothing more. He was worried for his girls. Sasha had picked up more hours at work and barely had time to spend with them as a family. Now he knew what she was feeling when he would be out late.

"Sasha can you come in here so we can talk?" Brandon called from the kitchen. Sasha was in the living room, watching a T.V show with the girls for the first time in weeks. He knew that she was going to be leaving for the night. It was Saturday, and from what he knew, girls' night was still going on. It was just that now Sasha no longer hosted the antics at their house when it was her turn. She told him that she wanted to be able to give him and the girls privacy for them to do whatever they wanted without her and her girls being in the way.

"Talk about what, Brandon? I'm trying to spend some time with the girls before I head out for girls night," she responded as she walked into the kitchen.

Brandon looked at her from head to toe. She was dressed in black distressed jeans with a gold silk blouse and black Red Bottom heels. His eyebrows raised at the sight of the new expensive shoes.

"Where did you get the shoes from?" He asked.

"Is that what you wanted to talk about? I told you I found them at a Goodwill last week. That's how I know you haven't been listening to anything that I say."

"Did you tell me?" He tried to remember the conversations that they had last week, and he honestly couldn't remember having any conversation about her new pair of shoes.

"Yes, I did."

"I don't remember. And no, that is not why I wanted to talk to you. Is there something that you need to tell me?"

A look of fear crossed Sasha's face but left just as quickly as it had come. She said, "No."

"Are you sure? Because it seems like you're spending more time away from home."

"Yeah, to make more money."

"And it seems like your attitude has changed. You're more arrogant than I remember you being."

Sasha sighed. This was not what she wanted to have a conversation about before she went to go see Nas. Whenever she would get into it with Brandon, it seemed like her attitude would carry over to her visit with Nas. To her, it wasn't the right thing to do because Nas had done nothing wrong to her.

"I'm thriving in my career and finally making as much as the men do at my job. I may be feeling myself a little bit, but that doesn't equate to me being arrogant."

"I beg to differ. Anyhow, I believe that there is something serious going on. Maybe you are having a mid-life crisis or something. I just would like it if you started to make time for the family. If not for me, then for them girls. They ask every night why you aren't home, and to tell them you are working is making them feel like you'd rather put work first."

Sasha rolled her eyes, placed one hand on her hip, and the other on the island that separated them. She spoke maliciously, "If that was the case, they are both old enough to express that to me themselves. So why haven't they? Is it them, or is it you?"

"Dammit, Sasha, stop being so fucking defensive. You got on my ass about being at work all of the time. I've stopped working so much. Now you are doing the same thing, and I'm asking you to cut back on some of the hours."

"And if I don't? What you gonna do? Leave? Nah, you won't do that. And you know why you won't do that?"

"Why won't I? You don't have time for us no more, Sasha. How much begging do I have to do in order for you to keep your ass home?"

"You ain't got to beg and do shit. You won't leave because you know that I know that you were cheating. You were just so crafty with hiding it, that I never found any proof. That's the difference between us. While you were sticking your dick in whatever bitch you was cheating with, I was at home, cooking cleaning, taking care of the girls, and working. Now it's your turn to experience how I felt. I'm not out here giving away pussy, I'm working." Sasha stated. She was done with the conversation and she turned to walk away from her husband. She hated to lie, but she had to do what she had to do.

She grabbed her jacket from the door. Ignoring Brandon calling her name, she walked out of the door and to her car. She was fuming. He had a lot of nerve. She reached into her purse and grabbed her cell phone as she put her car in reverse and began to dial Jade's phone number. When she had gotten the voicemail, she remember that they all turned their backs on her and weren't speaking with her. She threw her phone into the passenger seat and screamed in frustration. The only person that she had to talk to was Nas. Finding comfort in that, she put the petal to the metal and made her way to his house. She knew he was gonna have a meal cooked, some good wine, a listening ear, and some amazing dick to sling her way.

Time flew by when Sasha got to Nas' house. To Sasha, there was never enough time in the day to spend time with Nasir. When she arrived, she decided that she would leave her home problems at the door and focus on him. It was she who catered to him. She cooked dinner, she ran him a bath, she massaged his body, and she fucked him while making his toes curl.

It was almost two in the morning when Sasha's thoughts began to get the best of her. Guilt set in, as usual, and she was ready to run home. This time, she replayed the conversation she had with her husband before she left and decided to stay.

"What's on your mind, sweetheart?" Nas asked. They were laying on their backs and Sasha's head was resting in the crook of his arm. She thought that he had fallen asleep, and jumped when he began to speak.

"Just the usual shit," she admitted.

Nas turned onto his side to face Sasha and said, "Why do you do that to yourself?"

"Do what?"

"Make yourself feel guilty. You said so yourself that your husband was cheating."

"I don't have any proof that he was, Nasir. I was just accusing him because of his actions and the way he began to move. For all I know, he could have actually been working."

Nas laid back down and dropped the subject. He knew some things that Sasha didn't know but he didn't want to put it out in the open unless she was willing to be with him. Her husband wasn't what he was portraying to be, and he had all the proof that Sasha needed in order to leave him. He had to play his cards right. He stroked her face with his available hand and rolled over to face her again. He placed a kiss on her lips and sat up. He turned the lamp on and looked at Sasha.

"You know that I love you right? You know that I'm willing to do anything to make you mine right?" Nas rambled.

Sasha sighed as she sat up on the edge of the bed. She was tired of this same line of questions when she would come over. With the guilt that was weighting on her heart, she couldn't deal with his shit right at the moment.

"Yes, I know all of those things, Nasir, but right now I can't focus on that."

"What if I told you that I had proof of your husband cheating?"

Sasha's throat became dry. She paused in her movements. She listened to her heartbeat in her ears as she tried to comprehend what she'd heard. In a shaky voice she asked, "What?"

He climbed from out of the bed and walked over to his closet. She watched as he pushed a panel in and slid it out of the way, giving him access to a safe. After he punched in the code, he pulled a brown envelope from the safe and made his way back to the bed.

"In this envelope is all the proof that you need. Although you didn't need it because you are a woman, and when women feel it in their gut that their man is cheating, nine times out of ten, you are right. I told you from the very beginning that, when I want something, I go through whatever hoops I need to in order to get it. I did just that to make sure that I got you. I love you, Sasha, and I want you to divorce Brandon and move in with me with the girls. We don't have to get married right away, but we can work on that. You deserve so much more than what that joker is providing for you. If I give you this information, would you consider doing just that?"

Sasha sat there flabbergasted. The exact information that she had been searching for was right in her face. But what Nasir wanted her to do, would it be worth it? Would the evidence be damage enough for her to file for a divorce from her husband and be with Nas full time? Sasha sat on the bed conflicted by what was going on. She questioned if she even wanted to see what was in the envelope.

Nasir placed the envelope on the bed and walked out of the room. No doubt he was testing to see if she would look in it while he was gone. The envelope was burning a hole in her and she needed to know. Picking up the envelope, she cautiously opened it up and pulled out everything that was in there. The contents was mostly pictures and her mouth dropped at every last one of them. She couldn't believe what she was seeing. When she came to the end of the pile, there was evidence of text messages upon text messages between her husband and his mistress. At that moment, she decided that she would consider being with Nasir. Yes, she was doing what Brandon had done. But in her mind, Brandon had done the deed first, and she was getting her revenge.

Sasha placed the papers back inside of the envelope and placed it inside of her purse for when she needed it to confront Brandon. Her heart was beyond broken. Nasir still hadn't made it back inside of the room, so she made her way into the bathroom and cried her eyes out. Little did she know, Nasir was watching the whole time, and a smile formed on his face as he watched his plan unfolding. He was sure that it would be a matter of time before she would be in his house.

Mimi

Chapter Twenty-One
April Showers Bring May Flowers...And a Baby

Amekia was finally nearing her ninth month, and her belly poked out as if she was carrying a basketball. After her fight with Sasha, she took a leave of absence at work and decided to do everything she could to minimize her stress levels. She cut her friends off, and stayed home, only leaving to get food. She had done everything under the sun to keep her mind busy. She would read, watch TV, and even taught herself to crochet.

In the short amount of time, she had completed several outfits for her daughter. Since she didn't have a baby shower, she ordered everything that she would need for her daughter through Amazon and Walmart. Having peace of mind was the best feeling in the world, but there was something missing in her life that she couldn't help but to notice, and that was her girls.

This was the longest that she hadn't talked to them. And while she was trying to make sure that she was stress free, they still ran through her mind. She even thought about Sasha. Amekia had just let the delivery people out, after they had put together her daughters crib, and she sat on the couch. Picking up her phone, she tried Jade first, but didn't get an answer. Next was Carmen.

"It's about fucking time you called one of us," Camren yelled into the phone.

Tears brimmed under Amekia's eyes and she instantly felt bad. She mumbled into the phone, "I'm sorry."

"Oh no, don't cry, Amekia. I was only playing," Carmen responded, while kicking herself for saying something.

"No, you're right. I should have called one of y'all sooner, instead of shutting y'all out. I know that you and Jade have been trying to contact me, but that argument with Sasha just did it for me."

"Fuck that hussy, and the horse she rode on. She hasn't tried to contact anyone since that day."

"I figured that she wouldn't have contacted me, but you and Jade haven't spoken to her?"

"Nope. We chewed her ass out when you left, so of course, she wouldn't reach out to us. I don't know what's up with Jade either. I've been trying to call her for weeks now and she won't answer. Her car isn't in her driveway and the school said that she took a leave of absence for medical reasons."

Amekia gasped and asked, "Medical reasons? What for? What's wrong with her?"

"I'm not sure. The last time I saw her, she was fine. I spoke to her a few days before she just disappeared, and she was telling me that I needed to help her to break into your house to make sure that you were okay."

Amekia chuckled and then got serious. She asked, "If no one has heard from her, then how does anyone know that she is okay? This is why y'all should have listened years ago when I said we should have each other's house keys in case of an emergency."

"Damn, you sure did say that years ago."

"How does anyone know she's okay? If she left work for medical reasons, how do we know if she's not laying in her house dead? Did anybody think to send the police to her house to do a wellness check?"

"How do you think I know that she's not dead? I did that already, and they contacted me and let me know that she was fine. She smelled of alcohol, but she was fine. Our friend is going through something, and just like you did, I'm sure that she will reach out when she gets ready to."

Amekia couldn't stop herself from crying. In just a short amount of time, their group had broken up quicker than a 90's R&B group. Carmen tried to console her, but hearing her friend cry brought tears to her own eyes. Nothing needed to be said. They both cried for what used to be a sisterhood and wondered if they would ever be able to recover from this.

"Oww," Amekia moaned out. A sharp pain starting in her back and moving its way to her pelvis caused her tears to stop.

"What happened? Are you okay?" Carmen asked, drying her own tears.

"No, I don't think so. I just had a sharp pain in my back, and then it moved to my pelvis. I think it may be contractions."

"Oh my God. Denise. Denise. Amekia thinks that she's having contractions," Carmen yelled.

Amekia heard movement going on, on Carmen's end of the phone call. She was having slight discomfort but she managed to chuckle.

"Carmen. Relax. It was just one, and it could be a false alarm. Remember, I'm not even in my ninth month yet. Don't get yourself worked up. I'm not going nowhere until...ooooh shit. My water just broke," Amekia yelled into the phone.

"Denise, her water just broke. I need to get to her. Amekia stay right there, I'm on my way," Carmen frantically announced.

"You a bold face, bald headed ass lie. I'm calling an ambulance and going to the hospital," Amekia yelled and hung up the phone.

As carefully as she could, she walked to her room, grabbed her hospital bag and cleaned herself up as much as she could. She picked up her phone and dialed 911 for an ambulance. They instructed for her to lay on the couch and keep the door unlocked, and they would be there soon. She did what they asked and laid on the couch. Another contraction rocked her body as she looked at the clock that sat on her living room wall to track how long the contraction lasted. Several minutes later, Amekia heard the door being swung open and she prepared to be bombarded by the EMTs.

"I'm in here," she called out so that they could follow her voice to find her.

"Oh my God. Are you okay?"

"Carmen. How the fuck you get here before the ambulance?" Amekia asked in shock.

"She broke every damn traffic law getting here," Denise stated as she took a seat on the couch opposite from Amekia. Two minutes later, EMT's arrived and asked her tons of questions as they loaded her onto the gurney.

"I'm gonna follow you Amekia. I got your bag, and I'm gonna have Denise call Jade and Sasha so they can meet us there," Carmen yelled after Amekia as they placed her in the ambulance.

"Who should I call first?" Denise asked.

"Call Jade first. She's the baby's God mother."

***

For months, Jade had laid in her own filth. In the past two months, she had showered maybe a total of five times. The news that she received at the hospital had put her in a state of shock, and caused her to shut everybody out. She was done with feeling sorry for herself and decided that she'd take the liberty of getting her shit together, by first taking a shower, and then cleaning her house.

Time and time again, she wanted to pick up the phone and call Darion, but her tears and the ache in her body stopped her from doing so.

As she was cleaning her kitchen, her music stopped playing and her phone began to ring. Looking at the caller ID she noticed that it was Denise calling her. She knew something had to be up because, while they were friends with Denise, she never called any of them. She rushed to answer the phone.

"Hello?" She questioned.

"Bitch, get to Ellis. Your God daughter is about to be born," she heard Carmen yell through the phone.

"What? That's impossible, she still has another month."

"Well I'm following behind the ambulance right now. Get there now."

Jade turned her sink off and rushed to get ready to leave. She ran to her garage and climbed into her car, waiting for the door to raise up for her to leave out. Checking her rear-view mirror, making sure that she was clear to pull out, she saw Darion standing in her driveway. Her breath caught in her throat. She stopped her car and paused before she exited the car. Anger rose from the tips of her toes to the top of her hair follicles. She swung her car door open and stormed towards him, ready to attack him.

"What the fuck are you doing here?" Jade yelled. The tears freely falling from her eyes. As much as she tried to avoid him, she knew that this was something that needed to be done.

"I just wanted to talk to you, Jade. See how you're doing," he stated.

"You wanted to see how I was doing? Or you wanted to see if I got what you giving out?" She asked with her arms folded across her chest, trying her hardest to not knock his ass out.

His eyes grew big like saucers. There was no point in hiding his visit any longer. He asked, "Well do you?"

"How long have you known that you were HIV positive?" She asked with a shaky voice. She had just got to the point where she was out of denial and was going to accept her fate. She'd danced with fire, and now she just had to live with it.

"About two years now."

"What? Two years? Why the fuck are you just raw dogging females – I could fucking kill you and I just might. You don't deserve to live. Get the fuck away from my house, and if I catch you anywhere near my house or my job, I will make do on what I said, and your son will be fatherless, too."

Jade was disgusted. How can someone who is knowingly HIV positive just go around spreading the virus. He was handing out death sentences, and then acting like he was so concerned. As Jade closed her car door, she screamed at the top of her lungs. The pain in her heart was indescribable. She banged her fists against the steering wheel as she let out all of her frustrations. Over the last two months, she'd contemplated suicide, but got rid of the thought once she realized that Amekia was going to be giving her a God baby. With that thought stuck in her mind, she dried her eyes and made her way to the hospital.

***

"When will she be able to push?" Carmen asked the doctor. The doctor had just finished giving Amekia a pelvic exam to determine how many centimeters she was. There was a machine to the right of Amekia's bed, tracking her contractions, an IV pole, and a table with a pitcher filled with ice.

"At this point she is only three centimeters. Her contractions weren't close or strong enough yet for her to push. Whenever baby is ready to come out, that's when she will be able to push. Right now, we just want to keep her comfortable," the doctor stated. He pulled Amekia's sheet down, tapped her on her leg, and walked out, leaving Amekia, Carmen, and Denise in the room.

Boom!

The door to Amekia's room banged against the wall as Jade made her entrance. She asked, "What did I miss?"

Amekia giggled and responded, "Nothing. Except your god daughter making my water break and don't want to come out."

Jade made her way over to Amekia's bed and touched her stomach. She was in awe as she rubbed Amekia's stomach. She felt the baby moving under her slight touch. Her tears appeared again as she took Amekia into a hug and thanked her for giving her reason to continue to live.

Amekia didn't know what she meant by that, but soon she would. Over the next few hours, the baby slowly made her way down Amekia's cervix. Nurses came in and out of the room, giving Amekia an epidural. Sasha hadn't returned anyone's calls but had finally showed up close to midnight when the doctor had come in to check how far Amekia had dilated. All eyes were on her as the tension in the room between the friends could be felt.

"You are nine centimeters, it's time to push," the doctor announced. The room became alive as everyone moved around the room to get ready for the arrival.

"I came at the perfect time then," Sasha stated with a weak smile on her face. Amekia didn't care at that moment what the fuck was going on with them. She was just glad that they could put their differences aside and be there for her when it mattered most. They crowded around the top half of her body as the doctor and nurse instructed her when to push. An hour later, Amekia was exhausted and it seemed like her daughter didn't want to come out. The contractions were back to back but her baby wouldn't even crown.

"We'll give it a go again, but if she doesn't crown, we're gonna have to -"

Jade yelled, "Doc, I think I may see her head."

Going between Amekia's legs again, he saw that the baby's head was crowning. He got into position and instructed for Amekia to push with all of her might. Taking a deep breath, she placed her chin in her chest and pushed as hard as she could. Amekia saw Jade get excited and she knew that her daughter had finally stopped being stubborn and made her way into the world.

"One more push, and then she will be out. Push. Push. Push," the doctor coached. Amekia did what she was told, and then everything was still. The loud wails from the baby brought tears to all of her friends' eyes. And in that moment, she lived for it.

"She's here," Jade yelled excitedly.

The nurse held her up for Amekia to see, and Amekia couldn't help the tears from falling again. She asked, "What's her name mom?"

"Aziyah-Jae," Amekia beamed.

The nurses moved around, cleaning, weighing the baby, and cleaning Amekia up. The girls walked out of the room and waited in the waiting room in silence until they put Amekia in her room. An hour later, and she was settled in and the hospital staff gave them permission to say their goodbyes. One by one, they made their way inside of the room, making promises to see Amekia the next day. Sasha was the last to come into the room. The tension was so thick if Amekia had a knife, she could've cut through it. She decided to be the first to talk.

"Thank you for coming. It means a lot. I'm sorry about what happened at the restaurant," she said. She felt the tears coming, but she didn't let them fall. She had done enough crying, and she just wanted her friendship back.

Sasha thought about the words that she chose to use before she responded. She said, "I had a long time to think about what happened, and when it happened, I was sorry. I thought that maybe I should have been a little more sensitive to your situation, and I shouldn't have said the things that I said. Now that I'm here in front of your face, I do not feel the same. I came for two things, to see the baby, and to give you this."

Sasha placed the envelope that she had in her hands on Amekia's lap. Amekia looked at it before she picked it up and began to remove the items. She asked, "What is this?"

"While I valued our friendship, I never thought I would feel such betrayal. Those, my friend, are custody papers. I know you was sleeping with Brandon behind my back, and I know that you was begging him to give your daughter a chance. So, I decided to make that happen. Me and my husband will be seeking custody of your baby. Checkmate, bitch," Sasha stated with a sly grin on her face. She walked out of the room without looking back, leaving Amekia staring at the papers in a state of shock. As she cried, she thought, *Is this for real?*

To Be Continued…
Friend or Foe 2
Coming Soon

Submission Guideline

Submit the first three chapters of your completed manuscript to ldpsubmissions@gmail.com, subject line: Your book's title. The manuscript must be in a .doc file and sent as an attachment. Document should be in Times New Roman, double spaced and in size 12 font. Also, provide your synopsis and full contact information. If sending multiple submissions, they must each be in a separate email.

Have a story but no way to send it electronically? You can still submit to LDP/Ca$h Presents. Send in the first three chapters, written or typed, of your completed manuscript to:

LDP: Submissions Dept
Po Box 944
Stockbridge, Ga 30281

DO NOT send original manuscript. Must be a duplicate.

Provide your synopsis and a cover letter containing your full contact information.

Thanks for considering LDP and Ca$h Presents.

Coming Soon from Lock Down Publications/Ca$h Presents

BOW DOWN TO MY GANGSTA

By **Ca$h**

TORN BETWEEN TWO

By **Coffee**

THE STREETS STAINED MY SOUL **II**

By **Marcellus Allen**

BLOOD OF A BOSS **VI**

SHADOWS OF THE GAME II

By **Askari**

LOYAL TO THE GAME **IV**

By **T.J. & Jelissa**

A DOPEBOY'S PRAYER **II**

By **Eddie "Wolf" Lee**

IF LOVING YOU IS WRONG... **III**

By **Jelissa**

TRUE SAVAGE **VII**

MIDNIGHT CARTEL III

DOPE BOY MAGIC IV

CITY OF KINGZ II

By **Chris Green**

BLAST FOR ME **III**

A SAVAGE DOPEBOY III

CUTTHROAT MAFIA II

By **Ghost**

A HUSTLER'S DECEIT III

KILL ZONE **II**

BAE BELONGS TO ME III

A DOPE BOY'S QUEEN II

By **Aryanna**

COKE KINGS V

KING OF THE TRAP II

By **T.J. Edwards**

GORILLAZ IN THE BAY V

De'Kari

THE STREETS ARE CALLING II

Duquie Wilson

KINGPIN KILLAZ IV

STREET KINGS III

PAID IN BLOOD III

CARTEL KILLAZ IV

DOPE GODS II

Hood Rich

SINS OF A HUSTLA II

ASAD

KINGZ OF THE GAME V

Playa Ray

SLAUGHTER GANG IV

RUTHLESS HEART IV

By Willie Slaughter

THE HEART OF A SAVAGE III

By Jibril Williams

FUK SHYT II

By Blakk Diamond
FEAR MY GANGSTA 5
THE REALEST KILLAZ II
By Tranay Adams
TRAP GOD II
By Troublesome
YAYO IV
A SHOOTER'S AMBITION III
By S. Allen
GHOST MOB
Stilloan Robinson
KINGPIN DREAMS III
By Paper Boi Rari
CREAM
By Yolanda Moore
SON OF A DOPE FIEND II
By Renta
FOREVER GANGSTA II
GLOCKS ON SATIN SHEETS III
By Adrian Dulan
LOYALTY AIN'T PROMISED II
By Keith Williams
THE PRICE YOU PAY FOR LOVE II
DOPE GIRL MAGIC III
By Destiny Skai
CONFESSIONS OF A GANGSTA II
By Nicholas Lock

I'M NOTHING WITHOUT HIS LOVE II

By Monet Dragun

CAUGHT UP IN THE LIFE III

By Robert Baptiste

LIFE OF A SAVAGE IV

A GANGSTA'S QUR'AN II

By **Romell Tukes**

QUIET MONEY III

THUG LIFE II

By **Trai'Quan**

THE STREETS MADE ME III

By **Larry D. Wright**

THE ULTIMATE SACRIFICE VI

IF YOU CROSS ME ONCE II

ANGEL III

By **Anthony Fields**

THE LIFE OF A HOOD STAR

By Ca$h & Rashia Wilson

FRIEND OR FOE II

By **Mimi**

<u>**Available Now**</u>

RESTRAINING ORDER **I & II**

By **CA$H & Coffee**

LOVE KNOWS NO BOUNDARIES **I II & III**

By **Coffee**

RAISED AS A GOON I, II, III & IV

BRED BY THE SLUMS I, II, III

BLAST FOR ME I & II

ROTTEN TO THE CORE I II III

A BRONX TALE I, II, III

DUFFEL BAG CARTEL I II III IV

HEARTLESS GOON I II III IV

A SAVAGE DOPEBOY I II

HEARTLESS GOON I II III

DRUG LORDS I II III

CUTTHROAT MAFIA

By **Ghost**

LAY IT DOWN **I & II**

LAST OF A DYING BREED

BLOOD STAINS OF A SHOTTA I & II III

By **Jamaica**

LOYAL TO THE GAME I II III

LIFE OF SIN I, II III

By **TJ & Jelissa**

BLOODY COMMAS I & II

SKI MASK CARTEL I II & III

KING OF NEW YORK I II,III IV V

RISE TO POWER I II III

COKE KINGS I II III IV

BORN HEARTLESS I II III IV

KING OF THE TRAP

By **T.J. Edwards**

IF LOVING HIM IS WRONG…I & II

LOVE ME EVEN WHEN IT HURTS I II III

By **Jelissa**

WHEN THE STREETS CLAP BACK I & II III

THE HEART OF A SAVAGE I II

By **Jibril Williams**

A DISTINGUISHED THUG STOLE MY HEART I II & III

LOVE SHOULDN'T HURT I II III IV

RENEGADE BOYS I II III IV

PAID IN KARMA I II III

By **Meesha**

A GANGSTER'S CODE I &, II III

A GANGSTER'S SYN I II III

THE SAVAGE LIFE I II III

CHAINED TO THE STREETS I II III

By **J-Blunt**

PUSH IT TO THE LIMIT

By **Bre' Hayes**

BLOOD OF A BOSS **I, II, III, IV, V**

SHADOWS OF THE GAME

By **Askari**

THE STREETS BLEED MURDER **I, II & III**

THE HEART OF A GANGSTA I II& III

By **Jerry Jackson**

CUM FOR ME I II III IV V

An **LDP Erotica Collaboration**

BRIDE OF A HUSTLA **I II & II**

THE FETTI GIRLS **I, II& III**

CORRUPTED BY A GANGSTA I, II III, IV

BLINDED BY HIS LOVE

THE PRICE YOU PAY FOR LOVE

DOPE GIRL MAGIC I II

By **Destiny Skai**

WHEN A GOOD GIRL GOES BAD

By **Adrienne**

THE COST OF LOYALTY I II III

By Kweli

A GANGSTER'S REVENGE **I II III & IV**

THE BOSS MAN'S DAUGHTERS I II III IV V

A SAVAGE LOVE **I & II**

BAE BELONGS TO ME I II

A HUSTLER'S DECEIT I, II, III

WHAT BAD BITCHES DO I, II, III

SOUL OF A MONSTER I II III

KILL ZONE

A DOPE BOY'S QUEEN

By **Aryanna**

A KINGPIN'S AMBITON

A KINGPIN'S AMBITION **II**

I MURDER FOR THE DOUGH

By **Ambitious**

TRUE SAVAGE I II III IV V VI

DOPE BOY MAGIC I, II, III

MIDNIGHT CARTEL I II

CITY OF KINGZ

By **Chris Green**

A DOPEBOY'S PRAYER

By **Eddie "Wolf" Lee**

THE KING CARTEL **I, II & III**

By **Frank Gresham**

THESE NIGGAS AIN'T LOYAL **I, II & III**

By **Nikki Tee**

GANGSTA SHYT **I II &III**

By **CATO**

THE ULTIMATE BETRAYAL

By **Phoenix**

BOSS'N UP **I , II & III**

By **Royal Nicole**

I LOVE YOU TO DEATH

By Destiny J

I RIDE FOR MY HITTA

I STILL RIDE FOR MY HITTA

By **Misty Holt**

LOVE & CHASIN' PAPER

By **Qay Crockett**

TO DIE IN VAIN

SINS OF A HUSTLA

By **ASAD**

BROOKLYN HUSTLAZ

By **Boogsy Morina**

BROOKLYN ON LOCK I & II

By **Sonovia**

GANGSTA CITY

By **Teddy Duke**

A DRUG KING AND HIS DIAMOND I & II III

A DOPEMAN'S RICHES

HER MAN, MINE'S TOO I, II

CASH MONEY HO'S

By Nicole Goosby

TRAPHOUSE KING **I II & III**

KINGPIN KILLAZ I II III

STREET KINGS I II

PAID IN BLOOD **I II**

CARTEL KILLAZ I II III

DOPE GODS

By **Hood Rich**

LIPSTICK KILLAH **I, II, III**

CRIME OF PASSION I II & III

FRIEND OR FOE

By **Mimi**

STEADY MOBBN' **I, II, III**

THE STREETS STAINED MY SOUL

By **Marcellus Allen**

WHO SHOT YA **I, II, III**

SON OF A DOPE FIEND

Renta

GORILLAZ IN THE BAY **I II III IV**

TEARS OF A GANGSTA I II

DE'KARI

TRIGGADALE I II III

Elijah R. Freeman

GOD BLESS THE TRAPPERS I, II, III

THESE SCANDALOUS STREETS I, II, III

FEAR MY GANGSTA I, II, III IV

THESE STREETS DON'T LOVE NOBODY I, II

BURY ME A G I, II, III, IV, V

A GANGSTA'S EMPIRE I, II, III, IV

THE DOPEMAN'S BODYGAURD I II

THE REALEST KILLAZ

Tranay Adams

THE STREETS ARE CALLING

Duquie Wilson

MARRIED TO A BOSS... I II III

By Destiny Skai & Chris Green

KINGZ OF THE GAME I II III IV

Playa Ray

SLAUGHTER GANG I II III

RUTHLESS HEART I II III

By Willie Slaughter

FUK SHYT

By Blakk Diamond

DON'T F#CK WITH MY HEART I II

By Linnea
ADDICTED TO THE DRAMA I II III
By Jamila
YAYO I II III
A SHOOTER'S AMBITION I II
By S. Allen
TRAP GOD
By Troublesome
FOREVER GANGSTA
GLOCKS ON SATIN SHEETS I II
By Adrian Dulan
TOE TAGZ I II III
By Ah'Million
KINGPIN DREAMS I II
By Paper Boi Rari
CONFESSIONS OF A GANGSTA
By Nicholas Lock
I'M NOTHING WITHOUT HIS LOVE
By Monet Dragun
CAUGHT UP IN THE LIFE I II
By Robert Baptiste
NEW TO THE GAME I II III
By **Malik D. Rice**
LIFE OF A SAVAGE I II III
A GANGSTA'S QUR'AN
By **Romell Tukes**
LOYALTY AIN'T PROMISED

By Keith Williams

QUIET MONEY I II

THUG LIFE

By **Trai'Quan**

THE STREETS MADE ME I II

By **Larry D. Wright**

THE ULTIMATE SACRIFICE I, II, III, IV, V

KHADIFI

IF YOU CROSS ME ONCE

ANGEL I II

By **Anthony Fields**

THE LIFE OF A HOOD STAR

By **Ca$h & Rashia Wilson**

BOOKS BY LDP'S CEO, CA$H

TRUST IN NO MAN

TRUST IN NO MAN 2

TRUST IN NO MAN 3

BONDED BY BLOOD

SHORTY GOT A THUG

THUGS CRY

THUGS CRY 2

THUGS CRY 3

TRUST NO BITCH

TRUST NO BITCH 2

TRUST NO BITCH 3

TIL MY CASKET DROPS

RESTRAINING ORDER

RESTRAINING ORDER 2

IN LOVE WITH A CONVICT

LIFE OF A HOOD STAR

Coming Soon

BONDED BY BLOOD 2

BOW DOWN TO MY GANGSTA

Mimi